I0548964

Secret Santa

HER SPECIAL OPS SANTA

AURORA RUSSELL

Her Special Ops Santa
ISBN # 978-1-80250-526-9
©Copyright Aurora Russell 2022
Cover Art by Kelly Martin ©Copyright December 2022
Interior text design by Claire Siemaszkiewicz
Totally Bound Publishing

HER SPECIAL OPS SANTA

Dedication

First and always, this is for my own holiday-loving Santa and our two elves, through whose eyes I get to experience the wonder and joy of the holidays every year as if it were the very first time. To my friends, and one of my besties in particular for being an amazing, sassy and hilarious forever-friend. Also, for my dad and stepmother, for their unflagging support and love. To my brother and sister-in-law, and their incredible kiddos. Thank goodness all of you have a healthy appreciation for the absurd!

This story is also for my own hometown, where we made so many beautiful memories growing up. Finally, this is dedicated to the heroic men and women who courageously put themselves on the line day after day to serve, protect and care for all of us.

Chapter One

T.J.'s nose itched. It had, in fact, been itching like hell for over an hour, but he wouldn't scratch it. His cover was too damn uncertain, and he couldn't risk any movement until he got the intel he was waiting for. Instead, he deliberately relaxed each muscle in his body one by one, starting from the small muscles of his toes and going all the way up to his face and scalp, using incremental movements. After so long in one position, he needed to regularly ensure that his body remained limber, ready for action on a millisecond's notice.

I'm getting too old for this shit, he thought dryly, feeling the ache of every single old injury to his thirty-eight-year-old body. *Maybe I'll put in that retirement paperwork after this mission.* He tested out the idea in his mind and found that he didn't hate it. Then again, what on God's green Earth else would someone like him do? He figured he would probably be a lifer.

A couple of hours before dawn that morning, as his elite unit of Marines had been gearing up to jump off the side of their small ship to swim to their precarious positions, Bulldog had joked that they were getting to be dinosaurs in Force Recon years. T.J. had laughed it off — and Bulldog had always been easy to laugh with, lightening the mood of every mission since they'd gone through special forces training together with the rest of his unit — but now he wondered if his friend and teammate didn't have a point.

T.J. lay prone under scant cover in a shallow depression he'd hastily dug into the hard, rocky ground, coated in dried mud. It had been the only spot close enough to surveille his assigned section of the back wall of the U.S. Embassy that had become ground zero for the current terrorist uprising in the impoverished Middle Eastern country that had heretofore been relatively peaceful. Usually, he reveled in the thrill of the mission, the ever-present danger. He loved the feeling that came over him, the confidence that he would prevail over whatever awaited, that made him feel twice as alive. Today, though, he just felt itchy.

Without conscious thought — and after so many missions, it had become second nature, just another part of him, like breathing or blinking — he constantly scanned the landscape around him as well as the walls that surrounded the embassy. The heat of the afternoon bled into the slow cool-down that signaled the start of the dusk. In spite of the occasional loud noises from within, everything remained quiet from his position until he saw it…then again. *Yes*, there was the slightest movement behind the faint outline of a door built into the light, stone walls, coated with the dust that blew everywhere. T.J. continued to hold still, but he felt an echo of that familiar zing of excitement in his stomach. *This* was what he'd been waiting for.

Two figures, dressed in black paramilitary uniforms and toting what looked like older-model AK-47s, crept stealthily from the door. Actually, they were pretty good at being unobtrusive. In the waning light, with the lengthening shadows, someone else might have missed them. Not T.J., of course, but someone who hadn't had his training and mission experience. Not for the first time, he was struck by how painfully young the militants looked—like kids playing dress-up in uniforms. Armed kids, filled with rage, but with baby fat still in their cheeks. He didn't make the mistake of underestimating them, though. He'd seen that kind of mistake cost lives.

Oblivious to their audience, the two young men walked closer to him, and he had a moment's flare of unease that they might actually step on him, but they paused a few feet away. His ears practically twitched, and he couldn't believe his good goddamn luck when they started to speak. Their voices were low, but he was so close it wasn't even much of a strain to hear them. They spoke in the local dialect of Arabic, but he was passably fluent in several, including that one. It was one of the reasons he'd been chosen for this mission—why his whole team had.

"The Americans probably think we're too stupid to guard this door." The first young man's voice dripped with disdain, and he switched his weapon from one shoulder to the other, puffing up his skinny chest.

"It's not on any of the plans...and it is nearly impossible to see from the outside if you don't know where it is already. We wouldn't have found it if there weren't a traitor loyal to our cause."

T.J.'s mind raced. It was confirmation of what they'd suspected, and it wasn't good...but it certainly explained why it had seemed like the insurgents anticipated every move before the guards inside the embassy could make them.

The second speaker, who looked slightly older, grew thoughtful before he spoke again. "In fact, I think we should use it. We can set a trap for whatever rescuers the Americans think to send. We'll make it seem as though we never discovered the passageway out...leaving it look unguarded. But we'll have four or five men inside waiting to pick them off as they enter — the hallway is too narrow for more. It'll be a squeeze for five."

"We don't need five. Four good, strong soldiers and the will of Allah will make us victorious." In spite of the lengthening shadows, T.J. could see the light of fanaticism burning bright and feverish in the younger man's eyes.

"We may need only four, but five will guarantee that we bring death to all of them." The second man's smile was cold but then widened into something almost feral. "In fact, I love knowing that they will be so close to the survivors who barricaded themselves in the safe room, but we'll slaughter them like goats before they can reach the doors."

T.J. remained perfectly still as the two young terrorists stalked back toward the entrance, his thoughts chaotic. *Fuck*. They *had* hoped the passageway had remained secret so his team could use it to access the embassy. Still, it was better that he'd overheard their plans so they could anticipate and work around the ambush...and in fact, the info that there were survivors in the safe room was an added bonus. This situation was still royally FUBAR — fucked up beyond all recognition — but he and his team were elite operatives who only got sent in when everything was going to shit...or had already gone there.

As he was running potential scenarios in his mind, intending to remain perfectly still until full dark so he could make his way back to the rendezvous point and deliver his report, he heard the barest disturbance, nearly lost to the wind. It sounded almost like a heavy animal but...*not*. It took him a moment to figure out where it was coming from, and when he did, he swore under his breath.

What the ever-loving fuck is she doing?

The figure he saw emerging from the rocky outcroppings that led toward one of the poorer residential neighborhoods was unmistakably feminine, with soft curves and graceful movements. It was impossible to tell if she were American or some other nationality, but she didn't look like a local. Some of her clothes had dark brown stains, although if it were blood, it likely wasn't all hers if she'd been able to walk such a good distance, and she was clutching something to her chest. He silently willed her to stop, since her current path could possibly take her directly into the line of fire of the two bloodthirsty young terrorists he'd just eavesdropped on, but she persisted, and he had to admire her bravery...along with her beauty.

Holy hell, she looked sweet...like every dream he'd thought he'd long ago given up on, but what was a woman like her doing out here in the dry landscape of the back door to hell? And during a highly publicized terrorist uprising, no less? It was killing him to remain still. They were getting more cover by the second from the setting sun, so if she only paused for a minute or two, he'd be able to run to help her.

He couldn't help but twitch in spite of all his training and practice when he realized that what she held was a distinctive blue passport with what appeared to be the familiar glinting golden eagle. *Well, shit.* She was

American. When the orange-and-red glow of the dying sunset hit her face and showed traces of tears down her cheeks, he tensed, and something twisted in his chest at the idea of her being hurt. *Fuck it.* He wasn't going to wait until full sunset when she needed him now.

Rose Abbott had had an extremely crappy past thirty-six hours. First, they'd gotten the news at the clinic where she'd worked as a nurse for the past six months that a terrorist cell—one that had been growing in strength and violence—had somehow managed to take over the American embassy. That had been terrifying, especially because of how worried it made her for Alec. On top of it, she'd been forced to face the fact that her three fellow American aid workers weren't what she'd thought they were when a young patient of theirs, the sixteen-year-old wife of a much-older local businessman, had come in with clear signs of advanced labor and significant distress.

Rose tried to tell herself that she didn't blame Terry, Cal or Anne…and part of her didn't. It was some scary crap, suddenly not knowing if you could be a target anywhere you went, and she understood that they'd gone to flee the country as fast as they could. That had been her plan as well, before she'd seen Yemina…and the look of panic mixed with agony on the young girl's face. Yemina, and probably the baby as well, very likely would have died if she hadn't stayed there. The breech birth had been difficult, and she thanked God Yemina had arrived when she had, but then the hemorrhage afterward had been a full-on emergency. Thankfully, Rose had stopped the bleeding and administered a blood transfusion, but it had been touch-and-go for a bit. She'd thanked the stars for every second of her grueling ER, trauma and OB nursing training. She'd only been able to leave when the local nurse Yemina's husband had managed to hire – probably mostly for the baby boy – had arrived to take over ongoing monitoring.

Rose took a deep breath, nearly choking on the dry dust that swirled around her. She, at least, had known about the back entrance to the embassy that Alec had sworn her to secrecy on. Her colleagues had had no such luxury. As she thought her brother's name, a squeeze of dread clenched her gut. Was he all right? Had he been injured or killed during the attack on the embassy? Or was he even now waiting for her in the safe room, worried sick?

A movement from off to her right made her freeze, and she squinted her eyes to try to see better. Between the waning light and the haze created by the dust in the wind, she had trouble making anything out clearly. *Shoot.* She'd hoped to get to the back entrance before dark. In spite of the sometimes-scorching heat of the day, it got really cold very quickly out here at night. Her heart thudded nearly right out of her chest as an enormous figure emerged out of the dimness, and she would have screamed but he – and it was definitely a man – muffled any sound by putting one massive hand over her mouth. He wrapped his other arm around her waist and pulled her tightly against him, and her breath puffed out of her nose in short, panicked gasps.

She struggled against his hold, trying to bite his hand, to make herself heavy by going limp, then when that didn't work, by flailing like a wildcat in a snare, but the sound of his low voice near her ear stopped her.

"I'm so sorry to scare you, ma'am, but I had to stop you before you walked into the trap. I know you're American, and I'm a…friend."

His voice was deep and sensual, and his distinctly Southern accent so beautiful she could have cried. *Again.* Her hand tightened around the American passport that she still held. She'd gotten it out before heading to the embassy, thinking to display it if she needed to, but she realized she must have continued clutching it to herself like some sort of talisman until she'd forgotten it was even there.

Her brain told her to be wary. There was no reason the stranger couldn't be lying. He could be a mercenary, a human-trafficker, a traitor…any number of unsavory things. Even if her instincts told her that she could trust him, she needed to be cautious. She gave a minuscule nod of understanding that he seemed to feel against his hand or down his arm, and he grunted his acknowledgment.

"I'm goin' to take us back down to the ground, now, behind those rocks. If I take away my hand, will you promise not to make a sound?"

It was oddly intimate, him pressed so tightly against her that she could smell his sweat, the dirt on his skin and clothing and faint traces of his deodorant. His voice was a mere thread of a whisper in her ear. She gave her muffled assent and he slowly took his hand away from her mouth, so that she could suck in a deep—but silent—breath.

As promised, he tandem-walked them over to a nearby group of rocks, his movements shockingly fluid and graceful for such a big man. He eased them down to the ground with deliberation, until she was pressed to the rocky dirt, and he lay spread on top of her. *Covering me*, she realized. He was covering her from any gunfire, and he had been positioning his body even as they'd moved so that if shots were fired from the embassy walls, he'd be the one hit. Her heart clenched in her chest.

She took another deep breath, intending to ask him who, exactly, he was, but he stopped her with a gentle finger on her lips.

"No explanations…not now, not safe. We can move to a small cave soon, talk there."

She stiffened beneath his sizable bulk, her skin going icy with fear at the mention of a cave—a small, enclosed space for them to be alone…or maybe where accomplices waited. She'd been foolish to try him as far as she had. He was a stranger…more than that, he felt dangerous, menacing. If he were feline, and most men were housecats, he would be a tiger or jaguar. Her mind raced with plans to push him off her and escape.

His sigh was somehow nearly silent, but regretful.

"Hell…and now you're scared. How about if I give you a knife? Can we cut through the bullshit explanations and jump to you trustin' me? If they see us—catch us—we're both dead."

She turned her head and could only make out the profile of his face. His nose was very prominent, she thought absently, with a bit of a hook, and it looked like it had been broken before. *Not a charmer*, she mused, and it was oddly comforting.

"Give me the knife," she whispered, a mere breath of sound. She swore she felt him shudder behind her but thought she must have imagined it. As he shifted on top of her, presumably to take out the promised weapon, she felt something big and hard—and growing—press against the mounds of her ass, and she gave a small squeak of surprise before she could stifle it.

"Sorry," the soldier said, sounding chagrined. "You feel so fuckin' good. Can't help it. Just, uh, ignore it."

As if she could ignore something that felt that large…but he sounded so apologetic and embarrassed that she vowed to try to do as he'd asked. With a slight huff, he settled back over her, and pushed the hilt of a good-sized knife that she guessed would be well-maintained and well-used, into her free hand. She closed her grip around it and instantly felt more secure. First her father, then her brother, had trained her well in how to use a knife to defend herself. While the stranger might outweigh her and be able to overpower her, armed with his knife, she was confident she stood a good chance of doing serious enough damage to get away from him.

"Thank you," she whispered. She spoke so quietly that she worried he wouldn't hear her, but he must have had ears like a bat and gave a soft rumble of acknowledgment that she felt more than heard along her back.

In spite of the dangerous circumstance—in fact, maybe partly because of it—she felt curiously cherished and protected…safe. Weirdly, she felt the stirrings of possible attraction and arousal, which would be the height of foolishness. She ruthlessly quashed them and focused on reviewing the moves she would make if the stranger attacked her…although really, he hadn't had to give her his knife. He'd put himself at her mercy and, as he'd obviously hoped, it had helped her trust him.

"Feel better? Enough to let me take you to the cave?" His mouth was so close to her ear, she could feel his hot breath fan her hair and cheek. Goosebumps rose on her skin.

Am I willing to jump off the proverbial cliff with him and go to an unknown, secluded location? Rose squeezed her fingers around the hilt of the weapon, stroking her index finger up onto the side of the cool blade, and it grounded her. Still, she needed to remain logical. The knife could have been a calculated move to gain her trust and get her alone...but to what end? He already basically had her under his control. No...even thinking logically, he probably was what he seemed to be, some sort of dangerous, elite American security officer or special forces—yeah, special forces sounded right—and when she'd stumbled into his path, he'd done the honorable thing and saved her. In fact, he was probably risking his mission even now, and if she believed him about the trap, he was in much more danger with her than if he'd just let her walk into it.

"Your name?" she breathed.

He was silent and still for so long that she thought he wouldn't answer.

"T.J.," he finally responded, his voice terse for all that it was low.

"T.J.," she echoed. "I'll go with you, but if you try anything, you will bleed."

"Yes, ma'am," he whispered, and she thought maybe she detected admiration before he rose straight up like a silent wraith, displaying incredible strength, before pulling her to her feet and leading her into the inky black unknown of the night around them.

Chapter Two

She was incredible. She'd followed him through the dark, generally sure-footed but never making a sound when she stumbled, to the cave where he'd stashed his gear and planned to wait before making the meet-up time with his crew. All signals were currently being jammed within about a three-mile radius, but they would have gone radio silent anyway for fear of interception. They'd underestimated the insurgents before, and they wouldn't do it again. A lot of lives were at stake on this one.

She hadn't objected when he'd ordered her to wait outside as he went to check to be sure the cave was clear and hadn't been discovered. It was the perfect location, and he'd been lucky to find it—the entrance hidden until someone was nearly on top of it—but it would have been foolish to think that locals were unaware of it. The space was limited, and slightly damp, likely from the proximity to the sea, but when she'd entered as well, the space had felt positively cozy. She smelled faintly like perspiration—who the hell wouldn't after walking the hills for more than a short while? — and traces of what might be soap or shampoo, but there was also some elusive feminine musk that tantalized all his senses as soon as they were alone in the tight quarters. Instead of the gentle explanation he'd intended to give her, the kind reassuring words, what had he said?

"Stay here. I need to take a piss."

Real smooth, asshole.

Even now, outside in the surprisingly cold night air, the recollection had his face prickling until even his ears felt hot. After doing a quick tour to confirm that nobody else was close by, he splashed some cool sea water onto his face and neck, rinsing off the mud. It felt like heaven, and he soaked a cloth for the woman as well. He glanced back again at the entrance to the cave. He'd been keeping an eye out, both to ensure that no one somehow slipped past him to get to her but also to ensure that she didn't try to escape. He reminded himself that just because she appeared to be an American civilian didn't mean he could trust her. At best, she was a liability he didn't need. At worst, she could be working with the insurgents or connected to the traitor.

His body didn't care, though. He tried to remember how long it had been since he'd felt so strong an attraction for anyone, and he didn't know. Maybe when he'd been a young, dumb eighteen-year-old who was composed entirely of swagger and horniness, but...he didn't think so. It had been a dick move — his inner voice snickered — to poke her with his hard-on when he was trying to get her to trust him. He could get hard from adrenaline, but man, he'd found his intense attraction for the stranger as sudden and unexpected as it was unwelcomed.

"You're as dumb as a box of rocks, and you have the manners of a goat. If you didn't look so hot in your uniform, I would have left you years ago. I just can't pretend anymore. I met someone else last year. His name is Steve, and he's a doctor." Unbidden, Dina's parting words to him rose in his mind. *Shit*, he'd thought he'd banished them from his consciousness, but apparently his ex-fiancée's words were still lurking there, waiting to pounce.

"With your looks and personality, the only reason someone would want to be with you for longer than a night, T.J., is if you saved her life and became her hero." Dina's face had been filled with derision as she'd said that last, right before she'd slammed the door in his face. While he'd been gone on a mission, she'd packed up everything of value in the apartment they'd shared, including the large flat-screen TV and the goddamn king-size bed, then left him alone in rooms filled with cheap bookcases and a futon that his feet hung off the end of.

He shook his head. *Damn, more than a year later and her words still hurt*, he acknowledged to himself. And yet, he didn't know if he'd ever felt the same zing of attraction for his ex as he was feeling for a complete stranger—a stranger he should in no way get involved with since too goddamn much was at stake, a stranger he was going to have to lie his ass off to, even if only by omission. As he turned to return to the cave and felt a spring—a fucking *spring*—of eagerness in his step, he thought it was going to be a very long couple of hours.

She looked like she'd started to either nod off or maybe just slump over from exhaustion, but she straightened and became instantly alert when she heard him.

"That was a long piss," she commented dryly, surprising a small smile out of him.

"It was a long day," he returned, holding out the damp cloth to her. "Here... It's salt-water—can't waste any of the fresh—but it will still feel good on your face."

She set down the knife—*still within easy reach*, he noted—and took it hesitantly, swiping it over her face. Her sensual moan of pleasure practically echoed in the small space. "God, you're right. I didn't realize how grimy I was feeling." She rubbed the cloth on her neck as she spoke, and T.J. tried not to be jealous of the scrap of fabric.

Keep your mind in the game, Hook, he reminded himself, using his team's nickname for him when they wanted to rile him up...which was pretty much all the time.

"Um, did you just call yourself Hook?" the woman asked, her eyes both amused and concerned, and he sat down in between her and his gear pack, the size of the space forcing him to nearly touch her. Shit, he was probably dehydrated, making rookie mistakes. Thank Christ he hadn't said anything more compromising. He dug his water bottle out of the pack and took a long swig before handing it to her. She took a measured sip— and damn if his cock didn't twitch as she put her lips where his had been—but something about the way she swallowed led him to believe she'd been really thirsty, too.

"Hook is my unit's nickname for me, for that old 80's show...well, and my nose." He decided it was innocuous enough to tell her the truth about that, at least. She'd probably already guessed at least part of why some enormous American military type had been hanging out, hidden in the dirt, behind the occupied American embassy.

"I knew you had to be military," she answered, sounding pleased to have been proven right. "And I like your nose. It's…distinguished."

He almost guffawed, but then he realized from her shy expression that she was serious. Why did that make something in his chest feel warmer?

"I'm on a mission, and that's about all I can tell you, I'm afraid."

T.J. was a little wary of her easy nod of acceptance. He'd expected some sort of argument, and the lack made him unaccountably suspicious. Was she not asking because she knew who he was already? But that seemed far-fetched. And he'd already given her his knife, and she hadn't hurt him. She'd had plenty of openings. He'd made sure of it.

Of course, he'd never truly let his guard down, and if she were really, really elite, she would know that. She didn't seem elite, though. Her face, now cleaned of dirt and any makeup that she might have worn, looked young and vulnerable. Her lips and cheeks were a light pink that made him long to touch them, to feel how soft they probably were, and her eyes were grayish slate-blue in the dim light of the camp lantern from his pack. Her long, honey-blonde hair looked silky for all that it was in a messy, haphazard bun with wisps falling all over the place. She couldn't have been more than in her late twenties, and he would guess closer to twenty-five or -six.

Way too young for you, old man, he told himself. She looked fresh and innocent, even in the middle of what was fast becoming a war zone. He was jaded, experienced and felt so ancient most days, so tired, that he thought he might be going hard and numb.

"Can I see your passport?" he asked. It was a demand, and they both understood it.

She handed it over. "I got it out when I started to head for the embassy…thought I might need to show it to people to prove, you know, that I'm really American. I kind of forgot I was carrying it, I guess."

He raised his eyebrows, then turned his attention to her picture. It looked recent, like she'd just gotten her passport in the last year or so. Rose Abbott, born in Madison, Wisconsin. Something tugged at the back of his consciousness. Why did that name sound familiar? He was sure he'd never heard of her, though. He mentally stowed it to reexamine later.

"You proved it to me. What are you doing here, Rose Abbott?"

She looked uncomfortable, and he would guess that she was a terrible poker player. He reminded himself that that could be an act, too.

Unsurprisingly, she didn't really answer his question. "I'm a nurse. I work at a clinic nearby that is run by an aid organization, headed by an American couple but also staffed by locals. We had an emergency right after we got the news about the embassy, and I couldn't leave the patient until today."

"What was the emergency?" He didn't really need to know that, but he wanted to hear her talk about it.

"The patient was a teenage mother with serious labor complications. She had a hemorrhage and needed a transfusion." Her voice was both clinical and compassionate as she spoke.

Well, that explained the rust-colored stains on her clothing. It *had* been blood, just not hers.

"Where did the American couple go after the emergency was stabilized? Why aren't they with you now?" He didn't have to act upset. He was genuinely pissed off that the directors had apparently left her to find her own way.

Her eyes grew suspiciously shiny, and he took her hand without thinking. It felt small in his, but work-worn and a little dry...probably from so much hand-washing if she really were a nurse.

"They, uh, left before... They were afraid they wouldn't be able to get out of the country if they didn't go right away, but I just...I *couldn't* leave Yemina and her baby that way."

T.J. felt sick at the image her words conjured...of the directors and other staff leaving, while soft-hearted Rose was left on her own with a severely ill teenage mother. The fact that their worries hadn't been wrong — that all flights and routes of access to the country were now cut off and anyone who hadn't already left was basically stuck for the foreseeable future and likely to be subjected to violence if his team wasn't successful — didn't excuse their behavior.

"Of course you couldn't," he agreed, and she tightened her grip in his, leaning more into his side. He wasn't sure if it was a conscious or unconscious gesture, but it was satisfying to some deeply instinctual part of him that she was beginning to trust him, even if she didn't realize it. He hated that he had to continue to pump her for information, by any means that he could.

You won't mind if you get to put your hands on her, kiss her, touch her, a snarky little voice in his head answered. *You'd be happy to pump her for information – and for any other reason.* Yeah, his internal voice sounded like a fifteen-year-old boy sometimes.

"Are the mother and baby okay?" he prodded gently.

Rose nodded against his arm. "Yes, they were stable when I left, although still being monitored. The baby was healthy, but I worry about Yemina... Oh, shoot. I shouldn't have said her name...patient confidentiality.

I must be" — he could actually hear her jaw crack as she gave a gaping yawn—"super tired," she finished breathily.

"It has been an intense past couple of days," he agreed.

She tensed next to him. "Can you…tell me anything about what's going on inside of the embassy now? We didn't get any specifics in the news." Something in her voice made him think the question was more than just curiosity. There was some personal connection, he was almost sure of it. And she *had* been going to the secret back entrance.

He chose his words carefully. "There were a lot of casualties, mostly embassy staff and military who were stationed there, but they did let some of the civilian women and children leave." Yeah, he knew he hadn't imagined it this time. She'd visibly flinched when he'd said embassy staff and military had been taken out.

"Were all the staff and servicemembers in there killed?" The hope in her voice was painful, and he was pissed off that he needed to continue to pursue getting information from her. He'd so hoped he could rule out her being connected to the traitor, but some part of him had known that she still might be.

"Not all of them, no… That's part of why my team and I are here."

He felt like a real asshole when her face practically glowed up at him with hope and admiration.

"I'm grateful to you for saving me from walking into a trap," she said shyly. "I realize I, uh, never actually thanked you."

Her words surprised a bark of laughter from him. "No, I suppose you were too busy trying to fight me and threatening to make me bleed."

Even in the dim light of the small cavern, which didn't really reach any of the odd-shaped crevices inside, he could see her cheeks flush pink. *Damn, she's adorable*, he thought, and chastised himself for noticing. His time for pursuing sweet young things was long, long past.

"Thanks for not being offended by that, too. You could have left me lying out there in the dirt."

"Good to be suspicious," he grunted, then bit his tongue. *No giving advice to potential traitors and spies, T.J.* Still, he genuinely doubted she was either…but until he was certain, he needed to be cautious, for his brothers-in-arms if not for himself.

All in all, Rose was impressed by how well T.J. was handling having an extra liability around—and she was certain that was what she was, if not a downright suspicious character, at least in his mind. She knew she must be getting tired when she started to nod off against his shoulder. When he didn't shift away, she turned her face toward him and breathed in his masculine scent. It was warm and somehow still clean-smelling, in spite of how sweaty he must have been in the heat of the day. The trace of detergent was American—familiar and yet, combined with his essence, it was exciting.

"Did you just, uh, sniff me?" His discomfort, when he'd been so dominant, was endearing. "I can't rightly vouch for how clean I am right now." His Southern accent was more pronounced on that last part.

Leaning against him, feeling suddenly safer and more protected than she'd been in two days…*no, in much longer than that*…an odd lassitude stole over her. She was so exhausted she was practically delirious.

"Yes," she admitted. "You smell delicious…*'like good, clean dirt,'* my granny would have said." Her head felt too heavy to hold up, even a little, so she nestled it onto his shoulder. T.J. obliged by wrapping one massive arm around her, and she felt a jolt of awareness go through her. It was unexpected, especially since none of the other young men who had asked her out since she'd been working here had stirred so much as a glimmer of interest in her, but she just didn't have the energy to care.

"You're not from the city, I take it." He made the question a statement, but she answered anyway.

"No," she said dreamily, practically slurring her words. "A pretty little dairy farm...making artisanal cheese, butter, cream." Why was she talking about home? She never talked about it anymore, but she trusted him...even if maybe she shouldn't. "Near a lake, and when the wind blows, it's so quiet you can hear every leaf, every long blade of grass rustling...like a song."

"It sounds beautiful, darlin'." He sounded like he meant the words...wasn't just saying them. And the way he'd called her *"darlin'"* made her heart go a bit wobbly in her chest.

"It was...but it's probably all gone, now." The grief of the loss, so closely connected in her mind to the death of the grandmother who'd raised her, was still so fresh, so linked to thinking about the farm, that it felt physically heavy on her chest.

"Your voice is so sad," he commented, his low tone sincere, tender. He rubbed little circles with his callus-roughened fingers on her forearm and she felt the heat of his caress through the thin fabric of her cotton shirt.

"Sometimes," she admitted. "I miss it. We both do." She broke off, her heart pounding. The adrenaline from the alarm coursing through her body woke her up a bit.

Had he caught her slip? Miraculously, he stayed silent, and it seemed he hadn't.

"You left the farm to come here?" he nudged, but it was gentle. Still, she needed to be cautious. She couldn't get Alec in trouble for telling her about the back entrance to the embassy.

"Sort of," she hedged, and she didn't have to feign the enormous yawn, even larger than the last one, that practically cracked her jaw open with the force of it.

His low chuckle was deep and rich, filling the small space. She decided that for all that he was obviously rough and some sort of very tough, elite soldier, he couldn't be all bad...not with that laugh. *Right?*

"Why don't you grab some sleep while you can, Rose? I'll watch over you...and wake you before I have to leave."

"You're leaving me here?" She wasn't proud of the squeak in her voice. She was a strong, independent woman. She took care of others, was relied upon in truly horrific situations. She'd made it alone, on foot, through an unforgiving, dangerous landscape.

T.J.'s answer was matter-of-fact, and she appreciated it. "Only briefly. I have to be somewhere, and you wouldn't be able to make it without gear, even if I thought I could get away with bringin' you. I won't be able to stop you from leavin', but it's safest if you stay here while I'm gone. If I am at all able to do so, I'll make sure you get out of the country alive and well...although you only have my word on it."

It sounded oddly like a vow, then he was silent, as if giving her time to decide whether she believed him or not. It was silly, because she didn't really have much of a choice, especially if he was leaving in the middle of the night, but she appreciated it.

"Since you asked so nicely…" she tried to tease, but her words were interrupted by another yawn.

"Just put your head back down, close those gorgeous eyes and I'll keep watch. You can even hold the knife again if you want, like a lethal teddy bear."

He should have sounded ridiculous. She knew it. Instead, he sounded somehow charming. *Dehydration and exhaustion are making me loopy.* She put her hand back on the hilt of the knife and she felt his chest rumble with laughter as she laid her cheek onto it again. She'd thought fleetingly that she wouldn't possibly be able to sleep next to a dangerous near-stranger in the middle of what was now a war zone, but she'd barely even settled herself before she slid into the unconsciousness of deep sleep.

Chapter Three

Well, that was one shitty-ass interrogation, T.J. scolded himself. All Rose had had to do was tell him he smelled good, and he'd let her slide right on by without really even trying to get information out of her. She'd basically handed him the opening when she'd said, "*We both do,*" but he'd just told her to go to sleep. Oh, he could make the case that it was to gain her trust, to play the long game, but really…he plain old wanted her to like him. *No. No more.* As he sat there, trying not to move too much and disturb her — although she'd been so tired he would have been shocked if anything short of a bomb going off in their cave disturbed her — he recentered himself.

He was on a mission — a dangerous, covert and very important mission. His unit — *his brothers* — were counting on him. If he fucked this up, he could be putting Coop and Tiny, Jay, Frogger and Bulldog in danger. *And for what? So that Rose Abbott might look at me with that same admiration her eyes held earlier? If she isn't a traitor or working with a traitor, however unconsciously?*

No. It was his job to get intel…intel that she might have. No matter what, he had to get her to tell him how she'd known about the back entrance.

In fact, he ought to wake her up…but something still held him back. He told himself it was because he knew he'd have more time when he returned for her later. Sure, she could leave…but he really didn't think she would. If she were as innocent as she seemed, she wouldn't know where to go in the middle of the night, and even a total amateur would know it was dangerous to wander around in a hot zone. If she were playing a part, it almost certainly involved getting close to him, so it wouldn't be in her best interests to leave. He ignored the little voice in the back of his head that told him that he didn't have the heart to wake her yet when she'd been so plumb exhausted that she'd practically seemed drunk from it…that it didn't feel right pressing her in that condition. *Shit, maybe I should think about filling out those retirement request papers after all.*

When she shifted, adjusting the position of her head so that it rested more on the muscles of his chest than on the bones of his shoulder and turning her body farther toward him, pressing the soft swells of her generous bosom against him, he nearly groaned out loud. *This is like a slow, sweet torture*, he told himself, gritting his teeth against the pressure caused by the near-painful hardening of his cock.

It had been a long time since he'd been this close to a woman, and even longer since he'd made love to one. Unlike his ex, he'd been faithful…and it wasn't as if there were a line around the block of women hoping to stare at his ugly mug. He knew he had what his father had proudly called *"a character-building nose."* His manners had always been rough, but living for so many years from mission to mission with mostly just his unit to keep him company, he'd become harder.

Rose — *damn, even her name is sweet* — was a reminder of all the things he'd been living without...all the softness, gentleness, although he got the impression that her kindness was reinforced with a strong core. A weak woman would never have come here in the first place to work at a clinic for those living in the type of abject poverty he knew was common in the surrounding city and certainly wouldn't have stayed to help deliver a baby in distress at the potential cost of her own safety. *Unless she isn't at all what she seems*, he reminded himself.

When he returned from his rendezvous, he needed to get her to talk. She seemed to trust him, and more, she gave off genuine vibes that she was attracted to him. She could be acting in what she said and even in some physical reactions, but he'd seen the way her skin had flushed, her pupils had dilated and even felt the way her heartbeat sped up. He could still be off base, but even if she were acting to play it up, he would wager some of her attraction was real. If she continued not to reveal her source of intel, he would need to use that attraction against her, much as he hated to do so.

To his surprise, he found that he *did* hate it...but part of their orders for this mission had been *"by any means necessary."* It authorized them to kill but would also cover this type of action, for the greater good. If it fucked up his chances for any sort of real relationship with Rose — and why he thought that was even a possibility was beyond him, but a tired old jarhead had to have some dreams left — then Uncle Sam would be indifferent. Mission first, everything else later. He'd always agreed with that mantra wholeheartedly in the past, but now...

He looked down at her, at the rounded curves of her cheeks, covered in a golden downy fuzz, highlighted by the mellow camp light. In this position, the trace of something fruity — probably shampoo — was stronger, tantalizing him, and he heard a delicate snore, punctuated by the heavy, sighing breaths of someone who was deeply asleep. He'd almost forgotten, but long ago, the idea of protecting American innocents like her was what had motivated him to go into the Corps in the first place, where he'd swiftly been moved over to special ops. He'd wanted to be part of the line of proud servicemembers standing between foreign invaders and terrorists and women and children. Since then, he'd gotten bogged down in a lot of details and countless operations…but the quickening of his heartbeat and the way he unconsciously straightened his spine told him that he still felt that way — felt it to his bones. He could only hope she'd tell him without coercion…or if not, that she'd understand.

* * * *

Rose only vaguely recalled T.J. waking her up to tell her he was leaving. She'd known she should have roused herself more, asked questions, but she'd been so darn tired she had just listened blankly, nodding, then curled up again with the long-sleeved T-shirt he'd tossed to her when he'd put on his wetsuit. She thought he'd said something about giving it to her as a pillow. If she hadn't understood how tired she was before, the fact that she had mostly slept through the most attractive man she'd ever seen stripping down to his skivvies in an enclosed space, that would have told her. Even now, his scent, incongruously fresh in spite of the oppressive heat of the day before, clung to the cloth under her nose, and she inhaled it deeply.

She *did* remember that he'd said he would only be gone for an hour or two, tops. *If he comes back,* a sneering voice in her head added. *He already did his good deed in saving your clueless butt, and he has more important things to do.* As she drowsed, the thought turned over and over in her mind. He had seemed oddly sweet and patient, for all that he was obviously dangerous. She didn't think he'd just leave...but if something happened to him, she didn't think anyone else would know where to look for her. She had to come up with a back-up plan.

With that realization, her mind grew a little less foggy. Then she heard it. Faint, as if it came from a short distance outside, but unmistakable. Footsteps. Her relief that T.J. had returned, and more quickly than expected, was immense, swiftly followed by suspicion. *Why isn't he being quiet? And is he talking to someone?* She rose onto her knees, quickly clicking off the camp light, and knelt in the pitch black, straining her ears for any additional sound.

The noises that filtered faintly into the cave made her blood chill and her heart thump an erratic rhythm. She *did* hear a voice, but it wasn't speaking English. *Oh, God, someone else knows about this cave and is planning to use it.* That had to be the explanation. And she was a sitting duck. The truth made her feel cold and shaky as her mind raced, but she forced herself to take deep breaths and think logically — well, as logically as anyone could in this particular circumstance.

She hadn't seen a back exit, and T.J. had taken almost everything, including his pack and what had looked like a wetsuit, when he'd left. Her fingers groped for the knife, finding the reassuring hilt, but it would be a very wimpy weapon against more than one grown man. By the cadence of the footsteps, and the fact that they were talking, there were at least two and possibly three or more men. She quickly wrapped T.J.'s black shirt around her bright hair and pale face, to prevent them from giving her away immediately. Since she couldn't get out of the cave, she'd have to wait and use whatever element of surprise that she could. She decided that she'd hold completely still and try to listen to what they were doing in the cave. It was possible that they were innocents, just looking for shelter. *Possible, but unlikely*, the logical voice in her head reminded her.

Her Arabic was far from perfect, but she knew enough to understand a decent chunk of what was said…and the next words she could make out confirmed her worst suspicions. The men were talking about caching weapons in the cave, to use as reinforcements for the trap they were setting for American soldiers at the embassy. T.J.'s face, so simultaneously earnest and cocky, with his kind eyes, distinguished nose and stubborn chin, flashed in her mind's eye. *They're setting a trap for T.J. and his unit, and they're going to use some of these weapons to do it.*

This was really bad…and not just because she worried for T.J. and the others with him, along with everyone in the embassy. It also meant that whoever was outside of her cave was heavily armed and definitely planning to come in. Her only hope was to wait, still and silent, until the first man got all the way into the cave then to take him out with the knife. Having grown up on a dairy farm, she wasn't unfamiliar with the harsh realities of farm life, and as soon as she'd been old enough, Alec had taught her self-defense techniques. Still…

Could I really hurt someone so deliberately when I have taken the oath to heal? Her spirit shriveled a little at the thought, but she forced herself to think of it as protecting and defending everyone else. She tried to picture civilian embassy workers, some of whom she'd seen at the American Club with their young families, but instead she thought of T.J...the teasing drawl in his voice, the feel of his muscles underneath her cheek, the way he smelled like pure sunshine. If she failed and he came back to a stockpile in their cave, he'd be in grave danger, and she'd have no way to warn him—if she were even still alive. She thought maybe she could find the wherewithal to attack if she kept in mind that she was defending him.

As she waited, painfully still, for the first man to clear the cave entrance, every scrape of metal against stone made her flinch. Sweat broke out on her skin and some trickled in an itchy rivulet down her back, but she forced herself not to move. Her breath sounded harsh to her own ears, overly loud in the still air. The knife handle grew slick against her palm, and she rehearsed in her mind what she would do. Take one man quietly — she shuddered—just enough to incapacitate him, then wait for the second, and hopefully no third. She would take any chance at all to run.

She was concentrating so hard that she nearly missed the new sound, like an extremely quiet impact. The reaction, however, was instant and loud. Someone wheezed and another grunted, and pain laced the noises. There were sounds of rapid impacts of flesh on flesh, and Rose strained her eyes in the dark but she still saw nothing until a shadowy form entered, nearly imperceptible in the darkness. She tried to hold her position, but the man—and more than anything else, it was the sound of his breathing that revealed him to be a man—grew so close that she knew she had to risk moving or he would trip over her.

As soon as she scooted back, even though she tried to be stealthy, she knew she'd given her position away as he grabbed her arm with a punishing grip. She whimpered in spite of herself and heard a break in the scuffle outside.

"Rose?"

T.J.'s voice was a beautiful sound, but fast on the heels of her relief at hearing that he was there was worry for him. It sounded as if he were outnumbered and certainly outgunned. She opened her mouth to answer, maybe to yell a warning about the weapons, but the man's other hand clamped over her mouth and nearly blocked her nostrils as well so she could hardly breathe. Her sound of distress must still have been audible, however, since T.J. swore.

"I have your whore," the man called out in a harsh voice, and she wished she didn't understand him through his thickly accented English.

"Don't fucking touch her," T.J. growled.

"I will not harm her...much—"

Rose's blood froze in her veins at that, but as she tensed, she realized she still held the knife. *It's inexperience. You need more practice in combat situations,* her inner voice pointed out, and it sounded disturbingly like her brother.

"...if you release my friends and let us all go free," the man finished, and she was surprised his grip hadn't broken her arm. It felt like he was grinding the bones against each other.

"Not gonna happen," T.J. answered in a low, menacing voice that made the hairs on the back of her neck stand on end.

"Why do I not show you what I mean?" the man replied, a sort of desperate anticipation infusing his words, and he started to drag her so fast she nearly lost her balance. She managed to hold on to the knife, though, even as he pulled her through the cave entrance into the relative brightness of the starlit night.

In an instant, she saw that one man lay on the ground, either unconscious or pretending very convincingly. T.J. held a second man, and while a small cut on T.J.'s forehead and swelling on his cheek showed evidence of a struggle, the other man looked much worse for wear. His eyes were livid, burning with a dark hatred. She caught T.J.'s gaze as she made her move, going limp in the grip of the third attacker, the one who held her, and using his temporary surprise to slash out at him wildly.

He gave a shrieking yell that split the night before shoving her away from him, hard, so that she fell on a group of jagged rocks nearby. She twisted so that she wouldn't land on her own knife, and instead managed to smack her shoulder and head onto the ground, leaving the rest of her body to take the brunt of the rocks. She was so dazed that it took her a second to wonder why her attacker hadn't taken advantage of her position, but she saw that another man had emerged silently from the shadows, like a piece of the surrounding darkness that had just broken off and taken independent form. He took down her assailant with an ease that made her envious, securing him and moving over to the man that T.J. was still restraining.

A wave of relief passed through her so she felt nearly dizzy — *or is that just from the fall?* — and she had to close her eyes. When she opened them again, she was surprised to see the naked concern and tenderness in T.J.'s expression as he left the other soldier, who was obviously his ally, to run and kneel at her side. He masked the emotion quickly, so that she thought it might have been wishful thinking on her part, but his hands were exquisitely gentle as he touched her.

"Rose," he said, running his hand lightly over the exact spots where her shoulder and temple had struck the sandy ground. "What feels the worst? Did he have the chance to hurt you inside the cave, darlin'?"

She'd been strong throughout the past few nightmare days full of blood and tension, gnawing worry, then flat-out terror. She'd delivered a baby and saved a mother, been essentially kidnapped, and now taken hostage, all without breaking...not much, anyhow. But somehow T.J.'s tenderness, more than anything else, made the tears rise with a fierce intensity so that she wept uncontrollably.

"Ah, shit, baby...he hurt you. Where?" T.J. gathered her into his arms, sitting down on what must have been uncomfortable rocks, and lifted her onto his lap, against his chest, with a controlled strength that was breathtaking.

"Not...hurt," she gasped, the force of her emotions making her breathless. "Only minor," honesty forced her to huff out. "Just...too much...too much." In spite of her speaking nearly incoherently, T.J. seemed to understand, and the sounds he made were comforting, so that he was almost crooning a low, steady stream of nonsense as he rocked her gently against him.

She heard noises around them, stealthy but steady. She wanted to be stronger, to push away from T.J. and let him help with whatever his allies were doing, but she couldn't find it in herself to give up the comfort of his embrace for a few long minutes.

"I'm all right...so sorry for that. You can put me down to help your friends," she finally forced herself to say, even though she wanted nothing more than to remain on T.J.'s lap, enveloped in his arms, for the next week or two...or longer.

"No need," his voice rumbled under her cheek. "My friends work fast."

She heard a stifled snort nearby, almost as if it were part of the dark air around them.

"We won't stay friends if you keep slackin' off...but we got this."

Another disembodied voice sounded from her other side, this one with a faint New York accent. "See ya at the RV, Hook. You know what you have to do." She couldn't put her thumb on why, but the tone of this speaker sounded both grim and sympathetic.

"Lima Charlie," T.J. replied with a less-than-enthusiastic grunt. Rose knew from her brother that that was slang for 'loud and clear'.

There wasn't much of a sound, but something about the sudden stillness told her that she and T.J. were alone again.

"You okay to go back into the cave, honey?" T.J. asked in a voice that was so gentle and understanding that it made her want to start weeping all over again. She gulped against the lump in her throat.

"I mean, I'm not looking forward to it, but I'll survive...and I'm sure we need cover," she answered, forcing herself to be pragmatic.

T.J.'s arms tightened for an instant, and when he spoke, he sounded wondering. "You really are amazin'...the whole package."

It was a compliment, but she thought she detected a hint of sadness, too. No, that was wrong...maybe regret was closer. She didn't have more than an instant to wonder, though, since soon she was airborne in his arms and he was carrying her back to the cave that had seemed so cozy a short while ago, before it had felt like a trap. She shivered.

"Cold?" T.J. asked, not even sounding a little winded. Rose knew she was no lightweight—always tending more toward being what her brother teasingly called 'solid'—but T.J. could have been taking a slow stroll on a beach for all that her extra weight seemed to affect him.

"A little uneasy about there still only being one exit," she admitted, hating to show weakness but wanting to be honest.

He grunted what might have been an agreement. "We placed perimeter alarms a good distance away, so we'll have enough warning to get out in advance if anyone else comes by." In the glow of the moonlight, his face looked hewn from granite. She was surprised to feel a rush of affection. "That was why I almost didn't make it back to you in time, though."

He didn't put her down, but simply ducked to bring her back into the cave, mindful not to let any part of her scrape or bump the stone sides. When he'd again illuminated the small light and settled her into the corner, the slight disarray of the scant few items in the cave the only sign of her scuffle with the unknown attacker earlier, he settled back down next to her. He silently dug some supplies out of his pack, handing her a blessedly fresh-smelling cleansing cloth while he put a self-activating chemical cold pack on the place where her head had hit the ground.

When Rose was finished washing herself up a little, and T.J. had cleaned himself somewhat as well, she put her hand on his thigh. He seemed surprised when he flashed a look at her face.

"Thank you," she whispered, then again, more forcefully. "Thank you...for rescuing me before he..." Her voice cracked, and she couldn't finish.

"You don't need to thank me, honey. I'm just...so grateful I was in time. When I think what might have happened..." He sounded haunted, as if she truly meant something to him.

Warmth and that same unusual feeling of security swept over Rose, and she felt cherished as she hadn't been in a long time—maybe not since she'd been a little girl. "But it didn't," she reminded him gently, reminding herself, too.

Swept along by the feeling of safety, as if she'd known T.J. for much longer than she really had, she turned to cuddle against his side, under the thick, muscular arm that he'd draped around her. Like this, surrounded again by his warmth and scent, everything in her settled, leaving only heady relief and a rising heat of another kind.

"I believe you're a very kind man," she continued.

The small smile he gave her was rueful. "You might be the only one to believe that, honey, and for good reason. I'm not kind or gentle. Don't make the mistake of thinkin' I am."

"The kindness is well-hidden under your tough exterior," she acknowledged. "But I feel it."

"Maybe you bring out the best in me," he whispered, so low she wasn't sure she was supposed to hear it.

She studied T.J.'s profile, with his close-cropped dark hair, hooked nose, lips on the thinner side and ridiculously long eyelashes, so long they made shadows on his stubbled cheeks. Seized by some sort of wild impulse—or maybe just overwhelmed by intense relief that they'd made it through that last scuffle still alive—

she had to touch him. She leaned up the few inches that separated them and pressed her lips to his.

Chapter Four

T.J. stilled completely as her lips touched his, his mind reeling. He'd been marveling at how incredible she felt in his arms, as if she belonged there, and aching for what he knew he had to do. Her tentative touch had taken him by surprise, but at the sweetness of her mouth — *and how the hell does she manage to be sweet after all she's gone through?* — he was powerless to stop his reaction.

With a groan, he opened his mouth against hers, and gave himself over to the pleasure of the taste and feel of her. As he nibbled on her full lower lip, he took advantage of her gasp of excitement to stroke his tongue into her mouth, questing and caressing. He was tentative at first, but at her eager sound, he growled and began to devour her, pulling her against him and turning so he could face her fully.

Before he'd realized what he was doing, he'd lifted her to sit on his thighs, mostly out of the overwhelming desire for her to be comfortable. Still, the move brought the lush curves of her ass on top of his rising hardness.

With every squirm or slight movement, the friction was indescribable until he felt full almost to bursting. Her little gasps and mewls of arousal echoed in the small space, pushing his need to new heights until he thought she might drive him out of his ever-loving mind. He couldn't remember how long it had been since anyone had touched him like this, with such tenderness and innocent enthusiasm. *Has anyone ever touched me like this?* he wondered.

He'd initially hoped to keep seduction as a method for extracting information from her as a very distant last resort, although since he didn't think he could physically harm Rose, he'd had to keep it on the table but buried in the back of his mind. With this kiss, though, and her responsiveness, she had presented him with the perfect opportunity to pump her for information. He hated that his duty to his squad and to his country popped into his head, even at a moment like this, but he refused to let it sully the perfection of Rose, eager and responsive in his arms.

For perhaps the first—and only—time, he refused. He hadn't missed his team's subtle reminders that he shouldn't trust her, should do anything he needed to learn anything and everything she could tell him, but…this was a line he wasn't willing to cross with Rose. Maybe she was a master seductress, and he was only one in a long line of conquests, but if she felt only a tenth of the connection between them—if there was any remote possibility this could lead to something real, if he didn't fuck it up royally like he did everything else—then he wasn't going to tarnish her memories of this night that way.

Reluctantly, he drew away from her, ending the kiss and leaving them both panting. He felt like he'd run an obstacle course—a goddamned high-level course— with his heart beating like a drum in his chest. When she wiggled again, he had to grit his teeth or risk shooting off in his pants like a damn teenager.

"You don't owe me anythin', honey. I hope you know that." His words were strangled, but he congratulated himself for being able to speak at all.

"I know that," she answered. "I'm not touching you because I think I owe you. I'm just so happy to be alive, and safe and with you." She stroked his arm and he thought he might have trembled at the contact. "I know it's crazy, but you make me feel alive, T.J. I couldn't help myself… No, I didn't *want* to help myself." She said that last part like it was a confession, and something warm and new inside of him basked in the glow of her words, and the emotion that he couldn't deny behind them.

"*Rose*," he breathed, and the sound was both reverent and frustrated. "I'm tryin' to do the right thing, and you're killin' me."

Suddenly, she drew back from him, and he missed the contact immediately.

"Do you— Do you not want me?" Her voice was small, uncertain, and she kept her head bowed so he couldn't read her expression.

"God, honey…my God. I want you so badly that I'm achin' for you, and I think I might be dreamin' of your touch, the weight of your soft body on mine, for the rest of my goddamn life. Can't you feel it?" He shifted underneath her so that the spike of cock pressed into her, and her sharp exhale was nearly his undoing. He tipped her chin up with one finger, so hard with calluses he worried he might scratch her delicate skin. "But that's why I don't want to take any more from you now,

46

darlin'. I want everything between us to be freely given, with clear minds and hearts."

Her eyes were searching, and her chest rose and fell with her breaths, brushing against him distractingly.

And, *shit*, he'd revealed more than he'd meant to. He, Timothy Jefferson Browning, who had been so tight-lipped even with his own unit that they'd ribbed him about it, had just made more of a rookie mistake than he'd ever made when he'd been an actual Boot on his first assignment. He suspected Rose was too smart to have missed that, and he knew he was right when she narrowed her eyes, making a tiny line of concentration appear between her brows.

"Is there something you're supposed to get from me that I might not want to give you?" she asked.

His mind raced, and he knew he could handle this one of two ways. First, he could do what he'd always done, putting duty above all else. He owed his country—and his unit—total secrecy, loyalty and success at any price. *Living like this is why your sister's kids have nearly forgotten you, your fiancée left you for another man and half the time, you're not even sure you care if you come back from the next mission*, a little voice in the back of his mind reminded him, one that sounded a little bit like his conscience and his ex-fiancée combined. Second, he could try to find another path. No way was he betraying his unit, but he had wide latitude in how he achieved his objectives. Maybe he could tell a partial truth and still get what he wanted from Rose without screwing her over. It shouldn't have been, but suddenly, not losing their connection had become deeply important to him, even so that he could one day look back on this night with something other than shame.

Before the words left his mouth, he knew he'd decided on option two, God help him. "Do you trust me?" he asked.

"I think I've proven that I do," she replied tartly, and the contrast of her huffy tone with the fact that she was perched right on top of his hard dick made him want to chuckle.

"I find myself trustin' you, too, honey...more than I expected to, and certainly more than I should," he confessed, taking a deep breath. "So I'm gonna trust you to understand that I'm here on a mission, to save potentially dozens, hundreds or even thousands of lives."

She gave a nod of understanding, and he expected her to move from his lap. That she remained in his arms made something loosen around his lungs.

"Okay, then. Whatever you do or don't choose to tell me, or even whether you believe me, I want you to know that I'll do anything in my power to protect you and anyone you might be coverin' for, as long as it doesn't endanger my unit, embassy staff or civilians." The words fell heavily, and they should have sounded ridiculous, but he meant them, and by the way Rose's eyes widened, he thought she understood that.

"The insurgent group is in the secret back entrance to the embassy—the same one you were headed for. If someone told them how to find it, and someone told you..." He let the unspoken question hang there. "I couldn't help but notice you mentioned someone else...someone you were quick to skip over," he added softly.

As soon as T.J. had revealed that he needed something from her, although she'd tried to deny it to herself, Rose had known what he would ask. *Of course* he'd noticed that she'd mentioned Alec. Just as clearly, he would have known immediately that she shouldn't be aware of the secret entrance. If he was the secret elite operative everything about him screamed that he was, he must have been able to read her every word, every motion clearly.

He could have tried to coerce her with pleasure — and even now, her body was still crying out for more of his touches as if it had been set aflame by him in a way that she couldn't remember ever experiencing with her last three boyfriends combined — but he'd been honorable instead. In fact, she worried that he was risking himself by being so honest.

"Are you — ? Do you want me to forget that you told me that, so you don't get in trouble?" she offered impetuously.

His bark of laughter was like a pop of sound in the small, stone room. "God, honey, I wonder if maybe I got taken out by an IED after all and I'm lyin' in my bed inventin' you..." His voice softened. "But I'd never imagine you gettin' attacked and nearly hurt by those three rebels." He brushed his thumb over her lips, still extra swollen and sensitive from their kisses, making her shiver. "No, I don't want you to forget what I told you. I'm bettin' that I won't get in trouble — or not too much — but whatever happens, it's worth it."

Can I tell him about Alec? she considered. *Can I truly trust him? But haven't I already shown that I trust him that far?* She desperately wanted to believe T.J., so desperately that it made her suspicious of her own motivations. And yet, if he was who he said — and everything pointed to T.J. being a deep special ops operative — then he'd have no problem eventually finding the connection between her and Alec. They had different last names, since Alec had kept their father's name and she'd changed to her grandmother's after their dad had passed away and their mom left, but it was only a matter of time. This way, at worst, she was speeding up the process. At best, T.J. could help protect her brother from potential repercussions.

"I have a brother," she blurted out before she could second-guess her decision.

T.J. remained silent, waiting, until she worked up the courage to continue. He stroked her hip with one of his large, hard hands, but the gesture felt comforting more than sexual.

"He works in the embassy...or he did, if he hasn't been killed—" She broke off when a sob threatened to choke her, but she pushed it down. "He's the reason I came to the clinic here, specifically. He's older than I am, and our relationship has had its ups and downs, but I thought this might bring us closer together and...it worked." She took a shaky breath. "Last month, we heard rumors of an uptick in activity by one group in particular—religious extremists—and even though we hoped it would come to nothing, Alec told me about the back entrance to the building, but that I shouldn't breathe a word to anyone else."

"Shit, of course. Alec Barker is your brother," T.J. answered.

Rose's chin snapped up in surprise. "How do you know his last name?"

"Well, I could lie and tell you it was because his name was on our list of those with clearance—and his name is there, along with summaries of close contacts— but in fact, I can confirm that your brother was alive as recently as yesterday because I heard his voice on comms with my unit. He's tryin' to hold things together inside the embassy."

Rose nearly went weak with relief, the knot of tension that had been tightly coiled inside of her gut like a viper, ready to spring, relaxing just a little. "Is he…? Is it really serious, that he told me?"

"It's not ideal, but it also isn't strictly against his orders. We're allowed to communicate to civilians in times of crisis, so that's the view that I plan to be takin' on it…and the description I'll communicate to the head of my unit, who currently owes me a whopper of a favor for savin' his fiancée's life."

Unbidden, hot tears prickled Rose's eyes and in the back of her throat. "That's… Thank you, so much," she whispered. "He's all the family I have left."

T.J. squeezed her knee. "I'm not gonna lie and say that I don't want to do this because it's for you, but it's also the right thing to do. I took an oath, and I intend to uphold it until the day I die."

At his gruff tone, even as he confirmed that he held his duty above everything, she felt a wave of affection for him. She let her head and cheek rest on his firm chest, and he tucked her into the position more securely with his arms. She attempted to stifle an enormous yawn, but she knew she'd failed when the vibration of T.J.'s low chuckle tickled her cheek.

"Still tired, honey?" he asked.

"Exhausted," she admitted. "But I'm all worked up…like my heart is pounding and I want to crawl out of my skin, but I can barely lift my arms." She could only blame fatigue for what popped out of her mouth before she could stop it. "I wish…" She halted the words before she made a fool of herself.

"What is it that you wish, pretty Rose?" T.J.'s question was both tender and gruff. "It's just us, here, now... You can tell me anything. In fact, I'm declarin' that until we leave this cave again, the rest of the world doesn't exist, and we can only tell the truth."

She tilted her face up toward his without moving her cheek from his chest, reluctant to break the contact between their bodies, even for an instant. "Uh-oh, you might regret that when I spend the next half hour describing my porcelain doll collection in minute detail."

Even in the dim light, she could tell that his eyes sparkled and his lips twitched with amusement. "Bring it on, as long as you tell me what you wished, too."

Rose had never been someone to talk much about sex or attraction, so much so that as he was breaking up with her, her last boyfriend had told her she was cold and passionless. At the time, the comment hadn't even stung very deeply, since she hadn't felt much passion for him, and they'd both deserved better...more. Now, though, with T.J., a near-stranger, shrouded with secrets and half-truths, she was more turned on than she'd ever felt in all her twenty-six years on the planet. Perhaps it was the unique situation, and the intimacy created by it as well as the enclosed, isolated space, but she wanted to believe that they were in a bubble, apart from anything and everything else, where nothing could reach them, and there would be no consequences. *What would that be like?*

Swept up with the idea, she shocked herself by answering honestly. "I wish we hadn't stopped what we were doing...or that we could go back to that moment," she admitted. It was flattering how quickly she felt T.J.'s cock rise under her again. She couldn't help a small wiggle of her hips, and he bit back a moan.

"You're determined to force me to call on every ounce of the discipline I learned in my trainin', aren't you, honey?" he grated out.

"Yes," she breathed, and the word sounded wicked.

"I won't make love to you now, darlin', not like this…much as I want to, and *God*, do I want to." Even though he sounded genuinely regretful, her heart still ached. "But I would love to touch you, if you'll allow it?"

He suited his words to actions, brushing his fingers over her hair, her cheek and along her flank, down to cup one side of her ass possessively. Deep within her, she felt the same sensation of excitement, as if some part of her had been waiting for his touch, yearning, and now wouldn't be denied. It was joyful and heady, and she didn't know if she could have forced herself to refuse, so she didn't even try.

"Please," she whispered.

Chapter Five

That one word was all the agreement he needed to cover her mouth again, drinking in her distinctive flavor as he tangled his tongue with hers, pulling her so that her body was flush against his. She traveled her hands over his arms and shoulders, then played at the nape of his neck, her innocent touches inflaming his passion more than any more experienced ones ever had. Their combined breathing was ragged, reverberating off the cave walls. Every catch in her breathing, every quiver of her body, made him even more desperate to give her pleasure.

One thought kept echoing in his mind, that if this was the only chance he might ever have to touch Rose — and with the danger he faced constantly, not just on this op, but in every single one, it was always a distinct possibility — he wanted it to be spectacular for her. Even if he survived, Rose might return to her senses and decide that this — that *he* — had been a momentary folly, and he thought he could force himself to live with that.

No matter what, though, he wanted to be the man who lived in her memories forever, because even if she never touched him anywhere else, he was certain she was going to live in his.

Without fully knowing how she'd gotten there, he realized that Rose must have turned around, so that she straddled his lap, pressing her hot core against his length, hard and straining toward her. When she lifted her head with a gasp, the position also put the bounty of her breasts directly in front of his face. When he reached under her shirt to palm the soft mounds, tracing the hard points of her nipples through her soft, cotton bra with his thumbs, she rocked against him and threw her head back.

"You like that, hmm?" he murmured, and she nodded, wordlessly thrusting her chest toward him again in invitation. His laugh was low and sensual as he continued to rub her breasts, pulling the cups of her bra down so he could tease her bare skin. "Why don't you pull off this top and show me those pretty, pink nipples that I can feel beggin' for my attention?" he urged.

She flushed and held his gaze as she reached for the bottom hem of her shirt, pulling it up and over her head in one bold movement that seemed just like Rose herself...sweet as hell, but knowing what she wanted. T.J. groaned with pleasure at the glory she revealed.

"Beautiful, honey...so fuckin' beautiful," he breathed in admiration, the words hitching slightly as she shifted. Her folded-down bra held up the mounds like an offering to him, each creamy breast tipped with a rosy-pink nipple. "They're so hard, darlin'... Are they aching for me? Want me to kiss them for you?"

Her pupils dilated, and her breath quickened. Yeah, his Rose liked when he talked a little dirty for her.

"Y-yes," she stammered.

He frowned. "I couldn't hear that. You're gonna have to say it if you want me kissin' or suckin' or just rubbin'." He spoke so close to her that he knew his breath fanned over her skin, and he felt a shiver roll through her frame.

"K-kiss them," she gasped, her cheeks turning so red that they must have been flaming. He took pity on her — as well as himself — and bent to pull one hard nub into his mouth, making her cry out as her hands flew to the back of his head, holding him to her. When he reached up to gently stroke and pinch her other nipple, she made a sort of mewl of pleasure, and started to grind against him in a rhythm that threatened to shatter his control. He reluctantly released her nipple with one last, long lick.

"You're so hot, Rose... You feel so good against me," he said, the words strangled. "If you keep movin' like that, though, I'm gonna embarrass myself." He put the barest amount of distance between them and pulled his shirt off so quickly he nearly tore it at the seams.

"Lie down, honey," he urged, then kissed a trail across her chest. It was soft, like velvet, and he tasted salt on her skin.

Her expression was dazed, as if she couldn't think of anything other than his touch, and he felt a flare of masculine satisfaction. "Here," he offered, putting one arm behind her as he eased her down with the other, then gently positioned the folded-up thermal top under her head. He reached around and deftly unhooked her bra, sucking the nipple he'd neglected with his mouth earlier until he had her thrashing and moaning again. Next, he nibbled a trail down her ribcage and stomach as he worked at the fastening of her pants.

"T.J., that feels so good," she whispered. "*So good.*"

"Mm-m...I'm glad, baby, but I'm gonna make you feel even better," he promised, taking her mouth again and earning another sigh. When he had bared her lower half as well, though, she seemed to tense, and sat up on her elbows. Her hair was wild, her lips looked swollen from their kisses and the little bit of stubble on his face had left faint red marks on her pale, silky skin, so that she looked thoroughly ravished. His cock throbbed and pulsed until he longed to fall on her like a ravening beast.

"Wh-what are you doing?" she asked.

"I'm gonna taste this gorgeous cunt of yours, which looks like it's getting nice and wet for me, hmm?"

Her face pinkened again, even as her breathing grew more rapid. T.J. was confused for an instant until he put the pieces together. Nobody had ever done this for her before, but she was *definitely* interested.

"You don't have to, umm, do that," she said, trying weakly to push her legs back together.

T.J. thought his smile might have been more predatory than reassuring. "I know I don't have to, darlin'. I *want* to...so goddamn badly." He stroked two fingers along the length of her pussy, feeling how creamy she'd become. "Oh, yeah...so slick and ready for my tongue. Are you gonna let me drink some of that sweetness?"

He wasn't sure if he'd ever seen anything sexier than Rose, spread before him, flushed and ready. He held her gaze. "Don't forget. We can only tell the truth in this cave. I'm tellin' you I'm beggin' for a taste of you. So, Rose, do you want my mouth on your cunt, lickin' until you scream?"

A visible shudder ran through Rose's frame and goosebumps rose all over on her skin. *Goddamn it, she's fucking made for me*, he thought, flooded with a wave of possessiveness.

"Yes, oh, *yes*," she agreed breathlessly, letting her thighs fall open again in invitation. He settled so he was stretched out on the hard ground, uncaring of how unforgiving it was in his haste to open her fully.

T.J. started with small kisses on her mound, enjoying the feel of her soft curls tickling his cheeks, and inhaled her feminine, musky scent, incredibly sweet as she trembled against him. As he kissed, he petted her slowly, trying to get her more accustomed to the feel of him. When he could tell by the feel of her legs on his shoulders that some of the tension had left her frame, he gave a few tender caresses with his fingers, gauging her wetness and finding her nearly liquid with desire. With a grunt of satisfaction, he parted her folds to expose the inner petals of her sex.

"Such a pretty little pussy...and so wet for me," he groaned before lowering his head and covering her opening with an intimate kiss. Her taste was just as he'd imagined, tangy and sweet and all Rose. He couldn't recall any flavor he'd enjoyed more, and he lapped at the copious honey that coated her. At the first contact of his mouth, she jolted for an instant, then gasped when he slowly began to circle the nub of her clit with his tongue. When he carefully sucked the bundle with soft lips, still caressing it with the slightest pressure from his tongue, she bucked and went wild underneath him.

"T.J... Oh! Oh my God!" Her voice sounded hoarse, stunned. He hummed his approval, and she put her hands on his head — he thought unconsciously — to push him more tightly into the heaven of her pussy. He gave a low chuckle of sensual amusement, muffled by his position. His Rose was getting bossy. The feel of her nails on his scalp, mostly bare from his short haircut, sent a pleasurable tingle throughout his body, and his cock was so hard underneath him that he thought he could have drilled right through one of the stone walls with it. He shifted to ease the pressure, at least a tiny bit, and continued his attentions to Rose.

By the increase in her breathing, now coming in high-pitched gasps, and the way she arched and strained toward him, he could tell she was getting close. He loved every sound and frantic movement. As he slid two fingers back into her channel, which had grown so slick it made a wet sound, he felt her tighten around him. Then, when he curled his fingers upward, never stopping the gentle onslaught of his tongue, she made a sound that was somewhere between a shout and a whimper and went rigid before she shook with the force of her pleasure, her walls undulating around his fingers as the liquid spilled out of her.

He drew out her orgasm with small strokes and kisses until she finally went limp, only shuddering occasionally. He was so turned on by how she tasted, felt and sounded — especially now that she looked utterly spent, and well-loved, sprawled naked before him — that it took every goddamn iota of discipline that he'd ever possessed not to tear off his pants and bury himself to the hilt in her cunt.

The only thing stopping him was the recollection — and he forced his focus to it — that in a little while, he was going to have to leave. He couldn't give her any reassurance that he would survive the next twenty-four hours, and if he did, he and his unit would go on to the next hot zone. In the months that followed, he wouldn't be able to communicate with her openly, if at all. If he wanted a chance at something more with her — and *holy fuck*, he did, especially after learning the taste and feel of her explosive pleasure — he needed to earn her trust. He wanted there to be no doubt of his intentions, or for her to ever wonder in the long days ahead if he'd just been using her.

Her gusty sigh, filled with contentment, soothed something that had been raging inside of him, and recalled him to the present.

"That was…so…" She struggled to find the words, and he flattered himself that it was at least partly from the force of her orgasm.

"Did you like it, then?" he drawled, sitting up against the wall and pulling her back onto his lap, crosswise. He grabbed his shirt, too, and wrapped it around her.

"It was like nothing I've ever felt," she admitted shyly, looking up at him through her lashes. He bit back a groan when she shifted the tiniest amount.

"Are you… Does it hurt? Can I touch you?" she asked.

The Almighty himself is surely testing me, T.J. thought. *He's giving me the sweetest temptation I've ever faced, and I have to prove I'm worthy…even if it nearly kills me, and my dick.* "You don't know what it does to me to hear you offer, darlin', and there's nothin' — absolutely *nothin'* — I'd like more, but I want tonight to be all about you."

When she settled more firmly into his arms, even the slight pressure of the fabric moving almost sent him over the edge. "I could use a distraction, though, honey," he admitted, his voice strained. "Tell me somethin' beautiful."

Rose was quiet, thoughtful. When she began to speak, her voice, with a husky edge from her earlier screaming, was mesmerizing.

"My hometown is beautiful...which is a little funny for me to realize, but I guess I had to leave to appreciate how much I loved it and loved growing up there. It's nothing too extraordinary for most of the year, just another small town in Wisconsin, surrounded by farms and patches of beautiful woods and lakes. But at Christmas—" The pleasure in her voice was unmistakable...and the yearning.

"At Christmastime...really, starting with the second half of November, *nobody* is more festive than Hunt's Falls. We have a quaint little downtown, built up around the aforementioned falls, of course."

"Of course," he agreed, sharing her wry amusement.

"The town center is only about two blocks long and two blocks wide—we don't even have a single stoplight—but the city lights up every inch of the streets and the town square with these golden, twinkling lights, and every shop and business puts up an intricate window display. They even illuminate the fountain. It's so pretty... I used to make my granny and Alec walk the whole tour twice." Her voice held a bit of wistfulness, and he knew she was back in her hometown in her mind.

"It sounds glorious, darlin'. Tell me more," he urged gently.

"Well, there's a whole month of activities, like a winter parade—I rode on a float twice as a snowflake— a tree-lighting, carol-singing, horse-drawn carriage rides. But my favorite has to be the Christmas market. We used to bring our cheese there, and lots of other local artists and farmers would set up booths, too. People would come from all the neighboring towns and even from Madison and sometimes Milwaukee to shop there. The air smelled like roasting nuts and pine sap, from the wreaths and trees, and live bands would set up in the gazebo to play all kinds of music, but predominantly the kind that has a tuba." Her tone invited him to share her amusement.

"Obviously, the perfect music for a gazebo," he agreed softly, not wanting to break the spell of her words.

"When we were kids, our granny would get us each a hot chocolate with a candy cane, which we would drink super slowly to make it last, walking around to every single booth, admiring the work and trying samples of everything." She sighed, and it was filled with longing. "It was magical."

"Sounds like a little bit of heaven," T.J. answered, meaning it. Rose had painted such a vivid picture that it was as if they were far from the harsh sand and arid winds surrounding them, and the small cave had been replaced by a lively town square.

"It really was." She leaned her head against his bare chest. Even though her hair was mussed and wild, it still felt like cornsilk against his skin. "It declined a little bit when the town cut funding, but my best friend, Heidi, told me that it has been back and better than ever in the past couple of years." T.J. could hear the sleepy lilt creeping back into her voice. She trailed her fingertips absently over his chest, leaving sparkles of sensation in their wake, but he thought she might not even realize she was doing it.

"What would you do if you were there now?" he asked, partly because he just wanted to hear more of her lovely voice sounding happy, partly because he was halfway into the memory now himself.

"It's silly," she hedged, and the embarrassed undertone made his insatiable curiosity perk up and take notice.

"Ooh, now...I like silly. Is it something naughty, baby?" He couldn't think of the last time he'd felt so light, as if everything that he usually worried about incessantly, the life-or-death pressures of his intense job, the constant wariness, were being kept out by a bubble and he had nothing to do other than tease Rose and make her blush.

She bit her lip, and he longed to suck it back into his own mouth.

"Well, it's more romantic than naughty...but, a lot of couples do kiss, and bring a blanket." She definitely sounded tired now and dreamy with it. He found it adorable. He found *her* adorable.

"I could be very creative under a blanket," he answered, his voice going a little gravelly.

She giggled, and the sound was silvery, like sleighbells. "I have no doubt," she agreed.

"So tell me this silly, potentially naughty thing you've been pinin' to do," T.J. prompted again, surprised again by how badly he wanted to hear it before she nodded off again from sheer exhaustion.

"I've...I've always wanted to go on one of the horse-drawn carriage rides, but when I was a kid, it was too expensive, and when I got older, I never" — she interrupted herself with a huge, jaw-splitting yawn — "never had a boyfriend...willing to take me. I'd love to...go with you."

"Guess those Wisconsin boys really must be cheeseheads," T.J. murmured, stroking her hair back from her face. He noticed that his fingertips were so rough that the fine strands caught on them. He felt her cheeks stretch into a small smile against his chest and she mumbled sleepily.

"Sleep now and have sweet dreams, pretty Rose," he whispered, already aching for the moment that he would leave her.

* * * *

When she started to wake up, Rose didn't need to look around the small cave to know she was alone. The space felt empty and colder without T.J. It was crazy, but she'd felt safer, and closer to him in the brief moments they'd shared than she had felt with anyone in a long, long time. Maybe she'd never felt closer to anyone. She wanted to curl up in a ball and howl, but she forced herself to take several long, deep breaths. *He never made any promises*, she reminded herself. *You probably read more into it than he meant...so what if he didn't say goodbye. He probably had to leave in a hurry. You're on the front lines of what is quite possibly going to become the next big war.*

Still, all the rationalizing in the world couldn't prevent her from feeling hollow that he hadn't even tried to wake her as he left. When she rolled over, she realized two things. First, that she wore his shirt, which he must have slipped onto her without her noticing – so he very well might have tried to wake her and she'd slept through it. Second, there was a paper underneath her that crinkled. When she lifted it into the thin shadow of early-morning daylight filtering in from the mouth of the cave, she saw that there was a hand-written message in a neat, tiny script.

Rose,

You were so beautiful last night. You're even more beautiful now as you sleep. I have to go, and I'm selfishly leaving you here to keep you safe, even though I'm sure your nurse-y hands are itching to help the wounded. Frogger is one of ours, and he's keeping close to you. When we get the all-clear, he'll let you know, and if I don't make it, he promised me he'd tell you that, too. Don't freak out when you see the giant man in the black wetsuit approaching you.

I know I shouldn't ask it, but hell, I'm going to anyway. I want to see you again, to take you out the way you deserve. It's okay if you think I'm crazy or tell me to fuck off. I likely won't be able to call or write at all for at least a few months, but if everything works out, I'm hoping we can meet at noon on December 23rd, by the fountain you mentioned. I want to buy you a cocoa and hold your hand in downtown Hunt's Falls. Until then, I'll just be dreaming of it, and hoping you decide to come. No matter what, thank you. You reminded me what I'm fighting for.

Yours,

T.J.

The last few words grew wavy on the page, and Rose knew her eyes were full of tears. He'd felt it, too. He was so sweet, so wonderful. And he might, even now, be getting blown up or shot down. She hugged her knees to her chest and let her chin rest on top of them, sending up a silent prayer to God and any angels that might be listening to keep him safe, to keep Alec safe…to keep everyone safe.

She hated it, but T.J. was probably right to go without her. She wasn't a fighter. She might hinder them more than help when they initially went into the embassy, especially if they expected explosives or gunfire. Even with the knife that he'd left her—and she prayed he wouldn't need it—she was only decent against a less-experienced opponent. Still, she would be ready with the skills she could offer.

She stood, pulling on the rest of her clothes from the day before and packing up the scant belongings still inside the cave until she and T.J. might never have been there...might never have shared such warmth and bliss. *As soon as we get the all-clear,* she vowed to herself, *I'm going in to help as a field nurse.*

She didn't end up having long to wait until Frogger—who was indeed a huge man, with dark skin and eyes and an incredibly calm way of speaking—found her.

"All clear, ma'am," he confirmed, and she had to hold on to the rock next to her to keep from collapsing with relief.

"Any news on everyone inside?" she asked in a strangled whisper.

"Relatively light injuries on our side for today, ma'am, but some heavier ones from before," he answered, and she understood the undertone. Things had been bad before they'd arrived. She needed to brace herself for what she would find. Worry for her brother clenched again like a too-tight knot in her stomach.

"And T.J.?" she asked, almost afraid to hear the answer.

"Hook made it through fine."

Again, the world seemed to roar around her for a moment before she could pull herself back together. She forced her breathing and heartbeat to slow and remembered all the people inside who might be in desperate need of medical attention. She would be there for them, one patient at a time, just like she always was.

"I'm heading in, then," she said, feeling the familiar calm that descended over her when she was going into a tricky operation, something she'd learned when she'd completed her nursing rotation in the emergency room.

The ghost of a smile flashed across Frogger's face. "We thought you might. Already warned everyone to look out for you," he answered.

What she found when she arrived was chaos, carnage and a desperate need for her skills. She immediately started to work on several patients, guards and embassy staff alike, so that she was already well-established in the most sterile room that she'd been able to find to use as a medical area when her brother found her. Alec was dirty and banged up, but mostly unharmed, and she'd allowed herself a second to nearly weep with relief before going back to stitching and mending an endless stream of people. When the medical helicopters arrived, things became even busier so that she was kept busy for a solid twelve hours or more. When she was finally able to check in with Alec, he confirmed that there had been a small, secret group of US servicemembers who had infiltrated the embassy and ended the dangerous stalemate, but that they'd had to leave just as quickly as they'd arrived.

Chapter Six

Months later
December 22

"Thanks again for letting me stay with you, Hy...especially over Christmas. I hope that you'll tell Edie how much I appreciate it, too." Rose's gratitude was heartfelt.

"Oh my gosh! It's our pleasure...I'm so excited to have my best friend home, any day or week of the year." Heidi looked away from the empty road ahead for an instant so she could flash the warm grin that Rose recognized so well from the countless times she'd seen it over the twenty-something years that she and Heidi had been friends. "Oh, and Edie was so sorry she missed driving to pick you up, but she thinks things will be winding down with the Humboldts' calf soon, and she should be home for dinner tonight."

Rose waved her hand as if to push the very idea away. She knew that, as one of the few local large-animal vets, Heidi's wife, Edie, must be constantly on-call. "I, of all people, know that animals don't take a vacation, no matter what time of the year it is! That's one thing I don't miss about the farm...having to get up for milking at four-thirty in the morning every. Single. Day." She made a face and Heidi giggled. "I used to trade almost any chores with Alec to avoid having to do that subzero march, hours before dawn, to tend to the cows."

Heidi guffawed so forcefully that it made her messy chestnut bob shake around her head. "Yeah, I remember... Isn't that how your brother bamboozled you into mucking out the stables for, like, six months?"

Rose lifted one side of her mouth into a wry half-smile. "Seven. I did go through three pairs of boots, but I got my sexy biceps of steel in return, so I'm gonna say that was worth it," she said, before both of them broke into laughter again.

"Oh, holy crapola, I'd forgotten how amazing your arms were freshman year. You had definition like Madonna or — dare I say? — Michelle Obama. I was *so* jealous!" Heidi's admission set them both to giggling again.

When they'd gotten their mirth back under control, Rose turned to her friend, feeling a wave of warm affection. "It's so good to be with you again. I've missed you so much!"

"Same, bestie," Heidi agreed, and the late-afternoon light caught her brown eyes, turning them walnut-brown. Rose noticed that Heidi wore a fleece emblazoned with the name of the local agricultural lab where she worked under her characteristic bomber jacket. "Videocalls are great, but they're not the same...and not all of us can grow up to be jet-setters like you and Alec." She pulled a face. "Oh, fair warning, I wasn't going to weird you out with this from across the world, but since you're here, I figure you should probably know you've both kinda become local celebrities. The *Herald* published — I kid you not — a six-page spread on your heroic deeds in that embassy takeover. My mom framed it and put it on our portrait wall."

Rose groaned, but she could well imagine Burt Godfrey, the owner of their town's small newspaper, *The Hunt's Falls Herald*, being excited that two former Hunt's Falls locals had been involved in such a prominent international incident. Since the U.S. had continued to work with the democratically elected national government to restabilize the country, refortifying it against the small fringe groups of religious extremists, it continued to be a top news item on a national level. She had been proud to stay on with Alec to offer her medical services as part of the effort, but she'd continued to check U.S. news sources. "Oh, good Lord," she muttered.

"I'm personally totally okay with it, since there's finally something to top the four-page spread they did when Jonas was QB of the football team and they won the state championship in our division — although I do still have to see the sign about that win on the way into town every day," Heidi quipped. "You know he was insufferable for *years* after that."

"Um, you thought your little brother was insufferable for years before that, too," Rose reminded her friend.

Hy raised one eyebrow. "Fair point," she agreed, then her expression grew more pensive. "Seriously, though, I know you reassured me on our phone calls since then, but are you okay about everything that happened? Is Alec okay? Does your mysterious Christmas return have something to do with all this?"

Rose should have known Heidi would guess at least part of the truth. That was why they were best friends, after all. No matter how much time or distance might be between them, whenever they spoke or got together, it felt like they were two giggling teenagers again and nothing had changed at all.

"The takeover was really scary," she acknowledged. "I'm not gonna pretend it wasn't, but everyone was amazing, and the way that aid groups, military and local political and social leaders have come together in the aftermath has been incredible to be a part of. Alec was phenomenal...so brave and steady. He really wanted to come to Wisconsin for Christmas, too, but he's still stuck there, rebuilding. Without him holding steady at the embassy during the attack...the American and international response and damage could have been exponentially worse, and that's the truth."

The silence that stretched between them was comfortable, and Rose appreciated that Hy was giving her time to think.

"And yes," she continued, deciding to tell her friend something she hadn't mentioned to anyone else, not even Alec, although she thought he might suspect. "I met someone else there, during the takeover...an American operative. H-he saved my life, and we really connected...although lately it feels like it might have been a dream. He's supposed to be coming to Hunt's Falls...tomorrow."

If they hadn't been driving on the small highway that led from the interstate to their small hometown, Rose thought that Heidi would have slammed on the brakes.

As it was, her friend squealed. "Holy crap, that sounds like something out of a movie, Rosie! One of the sappy ones we used to sigh over at all our slumber parties!" She paused, and when she continued, she lowered her voice. "It also sounds mysterious."

"It *feels* mysterious," Rose agreed. "The more time that passes, the more I second-guess myself, wondering if I exaggerated everything in my memories, if I'm silly for even imagining that he'll actually show up, but, Hy...when we were together, it was like nothing else, like nothing I've ever felt for anyone before."

"So you're here," Hy finished. "You're being really brave, Rose, putting yourself out there. I know it isn't always easy for you to trust...having lost your parents so young, then your granny and the farm, too."

Rose hadn't thought of it in exactly those terms, but she realized Heidi was right. She never seemed to want to trust anyone enough to get truly close to her, especially not her last few boyfriends, and they'd all called her distant, aloof. But a part of her was always afraid of being let down...of waiting for someone who would never come home. It was easier to keep them at a distance or leave them first.

"And you haven't heard from this guy in, what, almost seven months?" Heidi prompted when Rose remained silent.

"Well, not officially," she answered, but she felt her cheeks heat, betraying her attempt at subtlety.

"Hm, now that *is* an intriguing answer. You know you have to tell me what you mean, right?"

Rose stifled a snort at the open curiosity she heard in Hy's voice and read in her expression. Her friend had never been able to pass up any sort of puzzle.

"So, I don't know anything for certain, but I did get a few random messages...and they weren't overly specific, probably because he couldn't actually put something that could identify him, but I'm pretty sure they were from him to me." Her cheeks went from warm to hot as she recalled some of the cryptic emails and texts, especially one where he'd talked about how badly he longed to hold her again, including what she thought was a veiled reference to her sweet taste.

"Um, why does your face look like a fire hydrant? What did he say? Like, I dream about your delicious magic pussy every night?" Heidi darted a glance at Rose, and her mouth fell open. "Oh my God! That *is* what he said! You little sexpot!"

"That's...that's not exactly what he said," Rose protested weakly. "He sort of...*implied* something like that, but he wouldn't come out and *say* it...if it was even him at all. I just... The messages sounded like him."

"Oh, ho! So he would *mean* that," Heidi answered. "I'm impressed. Go, Rose!"

"Hy!" she answered, torn between mortification and affection.

Her friend briefly took her hands off the wheel as if to make a don't-shoot gesture. "I'm not judging... I am the least judge-y person around, especially when it comes to talking about sexy ladies and love. You know what my favorite thing is to say on that subject?"

Rose narrowed her eyes. "Jam out with your clam out?" she guessed.

Heidi snorted, and it was a rich sound of amusement. "That, too... I mean, *obvi*. There's never a wrong time for *that* advice. But I was thinking more along the lines of *carpe diem*." The Jeep slowed as they pulled up in front of the pretty little split-level that Heidi and Edie had bought a few years earlier, which was fully decorated for Christmas with twinkling lights on every bush and tree in the front yard, gleaming even though it wasn't fully dark yet.

"If he was sending you messages when he could, it doesn't sound like he's forgotten you or that your time together didn't mean as much to him as it did to you. I think it's amazing that you're taking this chance, and I say, keep seizing the day, Rosie. No matter what, you're opening yourself up to love, and that's never a bad thing."

As they sat in the stopped car, Rose reflected that her oldest friend looked happy, and sounded like she knew what she was talking about. "You know, you're an awesome best friend. You know that, right?"

Heidi's smile was sassy, but her expression was genuinely pleased. "Does that mean you'll cook your famous vegetarian tater tot hot dish for dinner? Pretty please with a cherry pop on top?"

Rose chuckled at Heidi's hopeful expression, and her use of their childhood version of the saying. "How could I refuse, when you ask so nicely?" They stepped out of the vehicle together to make their way to the house through the brisk and snowy early evening.

* * * *

The next morning, the weather was perfect for December, and Hunt's Falls looked glorious with it. The downtown area was bustling, and everyone had a kind word for everyone else. There was just enough snow to make the place delightfully wintry, but not enough to actually be inconvenient. Rose loved the little bite of chill on her nose and cheeks, which she was sure were probably growing pink. She'd modeled her chosen outfit for Heidi and Edie, who'd agreed that the nice jeans and soft, flattering sweater struck just the right balance of pretty without looking like she was trying too hard.

She'd even put on the pearl earrings her granny had given to her on her sixteenth birthday, for good luck. If she were being honest, the special jewelry was also for courage. As she walked toward their designated meeting spot of the fountain — right in the middle of the town square — her heart was beating so hard that she thought everyone she passed must be able to hear it, and she was breathless with anticipation and excitement. Her hands, snug in the warm, woolen gloves she'd chosen, were suspiciously shaky as she adjusted her purse on her shoulder.

Rose tried to remind herself that anything could have happened, so she shouldn't get too excited, but her psyche was having none of it. Something in her chest and gut — something that felt like pure hope mixed with joy — refused to settle and grew stronger by the second. She looked all around the streets as she walked, scanning the crowd for T.J.'s tall form and distinctive profile that she thought she'd recognize anywhere, but there was no sign of him.

She felt almost as if she were floating — and maybe it was just lack of oxygen — by the time she reached the fountain. The surrounding park was busy, filled with families and couples, many of whom called out greetings to her, which she returned in a friendly way. She noted with satisfaction that the benches appeared to have been cleared of snow, and two teenagers were just leaving, having finished their cone of delicious-smelling roasted nuts from the nearby vendor with a mobile stand, so she was able to sit down. She watched the young pair absently as they meandered, arm-in-arm, heads bowed close together as if they shared a secret, and with a jolt she realized that that might be her with T.J. soon. She wanted it with a longing so fierce it took her by surprise. She couldn't wait, nearly bursting with excitement.

At first, she scanned every new arrival eagerly. When she dared a look at her phone, she saw that it had been twenty minutes. *Twenty minutes isn't so late*, she reasoned, *since I have no idea where T.J. is coming from.* After that, she bought her own cone of nuts — getting the large size so she could share with T.J. when he arrived — and settled to wait. They were warm and crunchy, coated with an irresistible salty-sweet crust, and she devoured a few more than she'd intended before she forced herself to reseal the cone and tuck it into her purse. She amused herself by watching everyone, taking note of the ugliest Christmas sweaters to recount to T.J.

Her high school math teacher, Mrs. Fleming, came over to say hello. Even as she kept one ear on the kind words the older woman was saying, on behalf of several of Rose and Alec's former teachers, Rose continued to surreptitiously scan the crowd for any sign of T.J. When Mrs. Fleming had finally hugged her goodbye, she was shocked to realize that it was nearly one o'clock in the afternoon, and her ears and nose — well, her whole face, really — were becoming uncomfortably cold now that a cloud had drifted in front of the winter sun.

Her heart sank, but she forced herself to remain optimistic. *I waited over six months*, she reminded herself. *I can handle T.J. being an hour late.* She pictured his note — which was carefully folded in her favorite book in her suitcase even now—the neat letters telling her that he would meet her here. Having come this far, she had no intention of missing him. She stood, stamping her feet, and turned a slow circle, looking at people and all the festive businesses. Her eyes alit on the bakery, which not only had a dizzying array of holiday goodies in the front window, but tables and a good view of the town square as well. She headed directly there.

Sitting down with a tea and a decadent Christmas-tree pastry that tasted like heaven, she resumed watching everyone hurrying around downtown. Whenever anyone opened the door, sleighbells rang out, which she found charming. A group of maybe eight kids who she thought might be high school students set up on the gazebo and started singing Christmas carols. *Good Lord, when did high schoolers start to look so young to me?* she wondered. When she'd finished her pastry and the last sip of the dregs of her tea, now gone cold, and the young carolers had finished their concert, she forced herself to look at her phone again. It was two-thirty. Still holding out a glimmer of hope, she opened her email on her phone…and saw that she had no new personal messages.

Her heart sank, and the food she'd just eaten felt like lead in her stomach. She needed to face the truth, that T.J. likely wasn't coming. She tried to repeat to herself all the logical explanations, which were the same ones she'd tried to keep in mind on her way. *Maybe he's stuck on a plane right now, or he couldn't get away from work. Heck, he might be in the hospital…or worse.* She hated to consider it, but given the type of covert operations that he seemed to be involved with—not that he would ever be able to tell her about them—it was a real possibility that something could have happened to him, and she wasn't sure if anyone would be able to let her know.

Or maybe he doesn't feel the same way you do, and the note and the messages were just some kind of joke, a little voice whispered in the back of her mind, sounding like all the popular girls in high school who had made such fun of her homemade sweaters and constantly dirty shoes. *Maybe he told his buddies about it, and they had a good laugh.* She wanted to discount that even as a possibility, but...what did she really know about T.J. after all? She didn't even know his full first name, much less his last name. He was like a ghost. Their time together had been so surreal that she might have convinced herself she'd dreamed the whole thing, if not for Alec confirming that he'd briefly seen some of T.J.'s team members, too.

In the time that she'd been thinking, another half an hour had passed, and she had to face the truth. Feeling like she was trampling the remnants of her heart, along with all her ebullient joy from this morning, under the soles of her boots, she stood and carried her dishes to the spot where the bakery collected them. Robotically, she returned the peppy holiday greeting of the young clerk, forcing a small smile. She barely remembered the walk back to Heidi's house.

When she opened the front door, Heidi and Edie's faces were excited, expectant. Their expressions transformed immediately when they saw Rose, though, and that she was alone. Heidi rushed forward to squeeze her into an immediate bear hug.

"Aw, Rosie...I'm so sorry," she whispered, and Rose could only hug her back helplessly.

Chapter Seven

It was nearly ten o'clock at night when T.J.'s transport landed in MSP—Minneapolis-St. Paul airport—and another five hours, between the car rental and the drive, before he got to a town even remotely close to Hunt's Falls. He was dog-tired, but worse, he was utterly heartsore. They'd been stuck on their last mission for an extra several days, and worse, it had been one where any sort of comms were completely prohibited, so that by the time he was able to retrieve his personal devices, they were dead. In fact, he'd only gotten them by special exception when he'd already been on the damn transport with no way to charge them, and no way to even attempt to let Rose know that he was still coming.

Maybe she didn't even show up, he told himself, and for a second, he almost wished that she hadn't, because picturing the alternative—her bright, pretty face, alight with excitement at seeing him again after so long, crumpling into disappointment—was almost worse. In fact, he didn't even know why he was still headed for Hunt's Falls except that he hoped that he'd somehow still be able to find her, if only to explain, then pray she'd forgive him. *How the hell am I gonna find her now, though?* he wondered. *Once she gets a good look at my face in decent lighting, she might run away screaming anyhow.*

He was unutterably weary, not only from the last op and the seemingly interminable trip back stateside, but also from the past six months. He was fucking exhausted, even amidst his friends and crewmates, done with the endless cycle of secrecy and violence, man's shocking cruelty and hatred for his fellow man. The light that had gotten him through, his beacon in the darkness, was the memory of Rose, and the idea — the *dream* — that he would see her again.

His eyelids were starting to feel gritty, and his skin was getting twitchy in the way he knew signaled that he was going to have to take at least a short break soon. He saw a sign for a cheap national motel chain, with a blazing neon *'vacancy'* on the sign. He was just pulling in when he heard a call come through the car's speakers. It startled him, but it shouldn't have. The first thing he'd done at the airport was to buy a new charger and plug in his dead phone, putting out the alert to all his crew. Someone must be getting back to him.

"Hello? Is this Hook?"

T.J. didn't recognize the man's voice on the other end of the line, which was so surprising that he almost ended the call reflexively. Even though the line was encrypted, nobody unexpected should have had the number and been trying to reach him now that he was officially on leave for six days…and if it were a stranger, they shouldn't know what his crew called him. The brass would have called him Lieutenant Colonel Browning.

"Bulldog called me," the voice continued, and something about it sounded familiar. The accent was somehow both military and Midwestern. At the mention of the nickname of the head of his unit, T.J. pulled his finger back from the 'end call' button.

"I'm listenin'," he confirmed, hearing the suspicion underlying his own voice.

"This is Alec Barker. I've only got about five more minutes before I have to head back to my post, so I'll just ask you straight up. What are your intentions toward my sister?"

The reason that Barker's accent had sounded familiar was because it was so similar to Rose's...although he sounded much more pissed off than Rose ever had. Well, except for when she'd warned him she would cut him with his own knife. Actually, she really did sound a lot like her brother, now that he thought on it.

"I don't believe that Rose would thank you for askin' me, but since I know how much you mean to her, I'll answer. I...*care* about your sister, very much, and my intentions are to take her any way that she'll have me. However, considerin' I messed up and stood her up not twenty-four hours ago, I suspect she might be takin' me at knife point and showin' me to the door."

The bark of laughter that came through the car speakers was deeply amused, and perhaps a little proud. "Threatened you before, has she? She's really good with a knife — taught her myself. A lot of people — men especially — take one look at her and think she's all sweetness and light, and she is those things, but she's strong, too. She's had to be."

T.J. hated that his missing their meeting might have caused her more pain. He fought the urge to curse. "I don't want to add to her burdens. I just want to find her so that I can make things right if she was waitin' for me and I didn't show." He meant it, too. When he found Rose, if she didn't want to hear his apology, or if she heard it and couldn't forgive him, at least he wanted her to know that he'd tried, so she wasn't left wondering. She deserved that...even if he longed to give her so much more.

"I have to go, but I've heard enough. I'll tell you the address of her friend Heidi's house, where Rose is staying. And I know she's still there because I spoke with her about six hours ago." The connection wasn't great, so T.J. couldn't be certain, but he thought Barker sounded, if not happy, then at least resigned as he gave a street address in Hunt's Falls.

"Because you and whoever you work with — and don't worry, I don't expect you to tell me and I won't ever try to look up your military record — because of what you guys did for us, I'm gonna give you something else. You can think of it as an early Christmas gift. I think my sister just might forgive you."

Some of the rigid tension in T.J.'s shoulder eased, just slightly, but it made a huge difference, and he realized that Barker had unintentionally confirmed even more. If Rose was in Hunt's Falls, she had definitely cared enough to meet him, and the fact that she was still there was also deeply encouraging. He felt like he could take his first full breath since he'd realized there was no way he'd make it to Hunt's Fall on time, and he'd had no way to contact Rose.

"Thank you...truly, *thank you*," he said forcefully.

"Just make it right," Barker said, his voice sounding more like a gruff dad than big brother, and T.J. realized that Rose's brother had probably had to be both for her. "But if you hurt her, I'll come after you myself."

If T.J. had been another man, he might have been more intimidated by the grim promise in Barker's tone. Still, he took the statement for what it was, which was pure protectiveness of Rose.

"Fair enough," he answered readily. "If I hurt Rose, I may just tell you where to find me."

Barker's chuckle was surprised. "Oh, and Bulldog said to tell you that the two of you are square now."

An unwilling smile spread across T.J.'s face. That sounded exactly like his squad leader, telling him they were even for him saving Lucy, Bulldog's now-fiancée.

"Copy that," he said, and the two men signed off. As he walked into the hotel, hoping fervently they had an open room so he wouldn't have to drive on farther tonight, he felt an unexpected spring in his step. Then he realized the cause...it was hope. He would rest, regroup, and go after his woman.

* * * *

"Rise and shine, buttercup!" Heidi screamed in her ear. Okay, well, fine, she didn't actually scream the words—more spoke them in a normal voice—and she wasn't that close to Rose, either, but Heidi might as well have been holding a megaphone for the way the words seemed to spike into Rose's very skull. When she opened her mouth to protest, she noted that it felt simultaneously two sizes too large and so dry that there might have been tumbleweeds blowing across it. A tiny little rattlesnake named Sid had likely taken up residence overnight...or a Gila monster named Petunia. At that precise moment, Rose might actually welcome a death by venom.

Rose gave a groan of pure agony and covered her head with her pillow. "Just let Sid and Petunia kill me in peace."

"Well, I don't know who Sid and Petunia are, but Edie and I aren't ready to give up and let the Grim Reaper have you yet—first, because we love you too much and second, because Alec would freaking annihilate me. Your brother can be a scary dude." Rose felt Heidi lift up a corner of the pillow, which had mostly been muffling her words...although not nearly enough.

"Finally," Hy continued, her tone becoming gleeful, "because you are a rockstar with an obviously very bright future in fairytale karaoke ahead of you, as you proved last night with your extremely creative and impassioned version—complete with interpretive dance—of the entire score of a certain animated mermaid movie."

At this, Rose sat up with alarm, the rapid movement nearly making her stomach lurch. "You're joking, right?" she said reflexively. *It can't be true...can it?* But then vague memories of holding a wooden spoon from the kitchen and singing her heart out into it as tears streamed down her cheeks filtered into her psyche, and she made a sound like a wounded animal.

"Oh, God, you're not joking." She answered her own question.

"Nope, I sure am not," Heidi answered unnecessarily...and did she have to sound so chipper?

Rose glared at her best friend from under her eyelashes until another horrible thought occurred to her. "Oh, Good Lord, I can never face Edie again!"

Heidi sat down on the edge of the bed. "Why, because now she knows how weird you are?" She made a face. "News flash, Rosie, she knew you were delightfully strange long before she met you, from all my stories about us. She thought you were hilarious." Hy's smile dimmed slightly. "Although neither one of us wanted to see you so sad and uncertain...but everyone has to let off steam sometimes. You've more than earned the right."

At the reminder of the events of the day before, Rose's chest grew tight with sadness and disappointment.

"It was silly, but I had really fallen for him, I guess, and I thought he felt the same way."

Heidi squeezed Rose's hand, and they both turned when there was a sound from the hallway.

"I bring offerings, but I can just leave them here?" Edie turned the statement into a question, and Rose could tell that Heidi was leaving it up to Rose to decide.

"Come in, please, of course," she answered, finding that she meant it. Edie was tall and strikingly pretty, with soft features and a kind smile. She was older than Rose and Heidi by only a few years, but she had an indefinable air of gravitas about her, as if she'd known sadness and survived. At first, Rose had worried that Edie might not be the best match for her outrageous best friend, especially since Heidi was so vibrant that she practically crackled with it. The more Rose got to know Edie, though, she realized that the two women were perfect complements for each other.

As Edie came toward her with a large bottle of sports drink in one hand and several pills of painkiller in her other, Rose decided Edie might be her new favorite person. She downed everything gratefully.

"Thank you." Rose knew it was her imagination, but she thought she could already feel the electrolytes from the drink working to help her feel better. "I'm so sorry… I don't drink very often, especially not champagne, and —"

"No worries at all," Edie assured her, hovering by the door as if uncertain whether she should continue or not. Something in Rose's expression must have decided her though, because she spoke again.

"I thought I might give you a totally unsolicited piece of advice," she said, surprising Rose.

"Please feel free," Rose answered, curious as to where Edie was going.

Edie looked at Heidi and something passed between the spouses before Hy tilted her chin as if to silently tell Edie to continue.

"I'm sure you don't know — because I asked Heidi not to tell anyone — but the first time she asked me out, I turned her down flat."

"What?" Rose couldn't help but ask, looking between the pair. That was not at all how she'd thought their courtship had gone.

Heidi nodded. "Like a duck being shot right out of the sky," she confirmed.

Edie smiled, and the expression was fond. "We'd been flirting at the gym for months, and we ran into each other at that coffee shop downtown — the Tuesday Blues. I really liked Heidi but, well, I had lost my wife to illness two years earlier, and…it wasn't the right time."

Rose was looking at Edie in an entirely new light. The woman must have been a young widow, and it was obvious she'd loved her first wife.

"As soon as I turned Heidi down, I felt terrible, and for two completely different reasons at the same time. It was like I was being torn in two, between not letting go of Melanie and denying the chance — the indescribably lucky chance — for second love that the universe had somehow granted me."

Edie came over to the bed and laid her hand on Heidi's shoulder. The look of pure adoration that passed between them made Rose's eyes prickle with tears.

"Well, as you can imagine, Heidi was respectful, but we stayed friends and eventually found our way back to each other. We usually only tell everyone that part of the story...but there was this other, painful piece of bad timing, miscommunication and plain old worry. If I had totally run away, or Heidi had given up on even our friendship, we never would have found our way to each other, and I'm thankful every day that we were both too stubborn and optimistic to let that happen."

Heidi kissed her wife's palm. "Me, too, Doc," she said, using the nickname Rose had heard Heidi call Edie before.

"Anyway, the point is that you said a few things about being disappointed and feeling like you wanted to give up on T.J. and love entirely. If he changed his mind or didn't recognize what a great person you are, then by all means, give up on him...but, Rose, you shouldn't give up on love. It's not easy, and it can be painful, but it is *so* worth it."

Rose's eyes filled with tears again, and when she looked at Hy, her friend's eyes had grown shiny as well.

"It means so much that you guys told me," Rose whispered, and they came together in a mutual group hug.

When they pulled apart, Heidi gave a wry laugh. "And here I was just going to make Rose get dressed and go back downtown for breakfast…to take the bull by the horns."

Last night, Rose would have sworn that she would have been too emotionally raw from her disappointment to go back downtown anytime soon, but after the pep talk from Edie and Heidi, she found she was feeling a little bit more optimistic.

"This has nothing to do with the fact that you think that the Bananas Foster French Toast at the Doggone Grille is, and I quote, *'the best food that has ever existed'*?" Rose teased.

"Aw, Rosie! If you feel up to mocking me, we're *so* going out for breakfast. You've always loved the Christmas festival so much that it would be a crime to let what happened yesterday spoil it for you. You have half an hour." Heidi's tone was sweet but firm. Just before she and Edie left the room, she turned back to add, "And I can't help it if the best French Toast that has been, or ever will be, happens to be in downtown Hunt's Falls, now can I?"

As she heard Heidi's and Edie's low laughter down the hall, Rose's chest felt curiously lighter. Deep inside, a little spark of stubborn hope persisted, and Rose decided that she refused to try to extinguish it any longer. She was going to remain open to whatever life decided to throw at her today.

Chapter Eight

T.J. was embarrassed to admit he'd overslept slightly. *Yeah, old man*, he chided himself. *You don't have the edge you used to.* Instead of waking up and checking out in the early morning, with plenty of time to find the house where Rose was staying, he'd been out cold until eight o'clock, which was practically unheard-of for him. To be fair, the op and travel he'd just finished had been brutal...but this felt like a shitty beginning for making things up to Rose.

Worse than being sluggish, he also felt curiously unsettled. He'd checked his reflection at least six times in the cookie-cutter hotel mirror, changing from one sweater to another, until he had finally recognized that he was nervous—really fucking nervous about what she'd think of his crooked nose and the wrinkles around his eyes from being too long in the desert, when she got a good look. It had been a long time since his stepdaddy had called him nicknames like "*fugly little freak*" and "*homely hillbilly*", and his momma had been too scared of her husband to do anything but laugh nervously. Billy Jericho might have been the first one to break T.J.'s nose, and the second, but he hadn't been the last. Things had changed, though, when T.J. had grown into the strong mountain of a man he was today, and by the time Billy had drunk himself to death, the tables had turned and he'd been afraid of T.J. instead — scared of what T.J. would do if Billy ever laid a hand on his half-sister, Candace. T.J. usually avoided thinking about that part of his childhood, or Billy, but today it was like he couldn't get the man's echoes out of his mind.

As he finished packing up the few items he'd taken out of his small bag, T.J. sat down on the bed. *Am I really gonna do this? What makes me think that I could be good enough for someone as pretty and sweet as Rose Abbott?* She'd risked her life for her patients at the clinic…and he'd heard more later about how fierce and tireless she'd been in the aftermath of the embassy takeover, helping to save countless injured before reinforcements could arrive. He'd been in awe of how tenacious she'd remained in the aftermath, too, staying on to help as the international coalition collaborated with the local government toward a more peaceful future.

Unbidden, the memory of her face, flushed pink with pleasure and satisfaction, rose in his mind. "*It was like nothing I've ever felt,*" she'd said about his hands and mouth on her. The recollection still filled him with savage triumph. The only thing better had been when she'd curled up in his arms so trustingly, confessing that she wished he would be the one to take her for the Christmas carriage ride she'd dreamed of. *Hell, yes, I am doing this.* He might not be worthy of Rose, but if she wanted him, if she could forgive him, he was going to take her and spend the rest of his days showing her how happy she could be—how happy *they* could be.

The GPS for his rental car routed him right into downtown Hunt's Falls, and it was just as charming and festive as Rose had described. The snow-covered trees and rolling fields, interspersed with rocky bluffs and several lakes as he neared the town had been beautiful—and so different from the steamy, marshy area of Mississippi where he'd grown up that it was hard to believe they were in the same country, much less the same time zone. The heart of the small town, though, was like an alpine village at Christmastime, decked out in all its holiday best. In fact, it looked just like one of the idyllic seasonal movies he'd noticed his little sister watching on a loop the last time he'd been able to spend Christmas with her.

As he scanned the busy sidewalks and storefronts, admiring just how incredibly detailed some of the shop windows appeared to be, even from where he sat in his car, he spotted something that made his memory spark instantly. There, right on the edge of the town square, was a café that had a beautifully chalk-drawn sign, complete with a steaming mug and candy cane, advertising their holiday hot cocoa. He hadn't intended to stop until he got to Rose's friend's house, but now, he started to reconsider.

He recalled that Rose had specifically mentioned how much she loved the hot chocolate at the Christmas market. In fact, he could practically still hear the remembered pleasure in her voice. *She would probably love a cup, wouldn't she? In any case, I can use any and all assistance with my apology. A peace offering never goes amiss.* Fast on the heels of his decision to stop was the worry that he wouldn't be able to find a place to park in the crowded downtown area, but as if fate were smiling on him directly, a parked car backed out right in front of him and he was able to slide into the spot, only a block away from the café.

Inside the coffee shop, the scent of fresh-roasted beans competed with the rich aroma of dark chocolate, and he inhaled deeply. It was odd, but the heady combination, so unique and delightfully familiar after all his recent travel, gave him the intense sense of homecoming. Silly, because he was such a wanderer that he obviously didn't have a home, but there it was. There were a few people ahead of him, but in almost no time, he was the proud owner of two decadent-looking peppermint stick hot cocoas.

Back outside, after the minutes he'd spent inside the steamy warmth of the café, the air felt positively frigid. As he started to walk the distance back to the car with brisk steps, he cursed the foolish vanity that had prompted him not to wear a hat or gloves. Just because he could handle extreme temperatures didn't mean he liked them, and T.J. was a warm-weather guy, through and through. He paused on the sidewalk, juggling both cups into one of his huge hands — 'mitts', Bulldog liked to call them to tease him — and flipped up the collar of his leather jacket one-handed, to better insulate his neck. He glanced up at the window of the closest storefront, which appeared to be a small restaurant or diner, intending to check his reflection in the glass. Instead, his breath caught in his throat at what — *who* — he saw inside.

At a table with two other women, half-facing him although not quite, was Rose. She was so lovely, just as gorgeous and vivid as he remembered, that he thought his heart might have stuttered in his chest. For a second, he couldn't believe she was truly there, so close to him. After noticing how absolutely stunning she was, especially in the warm light of the late-morning sun, he saw that she also looked a bit sad. She smiled at something one of the other women said, but it didn't quite reach her eyes, and the corners of her mouth turned down just a bit. *Did I cause that?* he wondered.

When she lifted her cup to take a sip of coffee, she froze with it halfway to her lips as she spotted him, her face registering shock, then something closer to hope. Their eyes locked for an instant that felt endless. In that moment, T.J. no longer heard the street noise and chatter around him or felt the brisk cold. He was so mesmerized by the soft expressions playing across her face that he thought he might have even tried to take a step forward until the window stopped him.

For her part, Rose seemed equally entranced. Without looking away, she put down her coffee cup and stood abruptly. T.J. wasn't sure how he managed to open and get through the restaurant door with both cocoas still in one hand, but he did, coming to stand close to her table, with only a few feet separating them. He was so near he could smell a hint of her shampoo and see that the sunlight was sparkling off the peach fuzz on her cheeks, making her look ethereal.

"You're here," she whispered, and for an instant, he thought she looked open…maybe even happy. But then she shuttered her expression, as if she were pulling back into herself. "I'm just glad you're all right." She sounded like she might mean the opposite, but he decided to ignore that.

He'd never been great at expressing his feelings, but he could tell that if he didn't do or say something, she was going to close off entirely. He took a deep breath.

"I'm so sorry, Rose. Truly. I hate that I left you waitin' and worryin' yesterday."

He felt the same electric pull of attraction between them, especially when she tilted her stubborn chin up in the air and looked down her nose at him like a queen.

"Thank you for that, at least," she said, her tone stilted.

His chest ached, seeing how he'd wounded her, but the way she'd greeted him told him that there might indeed still be hope. He firmed his resolve, drawing himself up to his full height of six feet and five inches.

"Maybe... Would you take a walk with me?" He gestured at the two cocoas he still balanced in one hand and noticed that one of the cups was looking a bit worse for wear. "I, ah, got you a peppermint hot chocolate," he finished, feeling so awkward that heat rose up his neck and spread to his face.

Rose's expression was a fascinating contrast between eagerness and reluctance, and she pursed her full lips so that he longed to kiss her.

He didn't need to look around to tell that every eye in the small dining room was on their table. Being from a small town himself, he was certain that most of the people in the place probably knew Rose, as well as her brother.

Someone close by made a small noise, and for the first time, he took a good look at the other two women sharing the table with Rose. One was short and athletic-looking, with a messy bob that made her appear as though she'd just been jogging in a breeze. She positively exuded action and attitude. He was reasonably certain she'd been the one to make the noise. The other woman was a little older, a statuesque beauty who gave off a calming vibe. They must be Heidi and Edie, Rose's friends.

"I think we're pretty much done here, Rosie, if you want to go with your, uh, *friend*," the smaller one said, her nonchalant tone belied by the spark of mischief in her dark eyes. "Edie and I can take care of everything. Take your time—no rush!—and just meet us back at the house whenever."

T.J. had guessed that she was Heidi, Rose's best friend, but here was the confirmation.

Something indefinable passed between the three women, as if they were all in on some secret, silent conversation. Rose bit her lip and looked so vulnerable for a second that he wished he had the right to just pull her into his arms and carry her off so he could love her until she forgot everything else.

"Well, if you're...sure?" Rose made the statement a question.

Both women nodded, and Heidi's movement was so vehement it made her hair bounce, resettling into a different wind-blown-looking configuration.

"Super-duper sure...go on!" Heidi answered, the Midwestern accent that had been faint before becoming more pronounced.

"A walk, then," Rose answered, and his heart leaped right into his throat.

His tongue felt almost glued to the roof of his mouth when she moved from behind the barrier of the table. She was that beautiful. It was almost surreal to be this close to her again in person after so many months of dreaming, of convincing himself she couldn't possibly have been as perfect as he remembered.

When she lifted her coat from the back of her chair and started to put it on, he hastily set the cocoas down behind him, much to the amusement of the old couple who shared the table there, unabashedly staring at the scene playing out before their eyes. T.J. took over from Rose, grabbing the shoulders of her thick jacket, and slid it onto first one arm, then the other. At the innocent contact of his hands along her back, the feeling of her so close in front of him, the hint of fruit he could smell as her hair shifted, his cock went instantly so hard that he almost groaned. When she gave him a shy smile over her shoulder, it was all he could to stop himself from backing her up to the wall and kissing her within an inch of her life.

"Uh, pardon me...sorry about that," he mumbled to the older couple as he snatched the cocoas up again.

"Oh, no apology necessary, young man," the older gentleman assured him.

T.J. put his hand lightly on the small of Rose's back, and even through the thick fabric of her coat, sweater, and whatever else she might be wearing, his whole body thrilled at the contact. *Damn, I hope I get to find out what she's wearing under her sweater.* As the stray thought popped into his head, he nearly stumbled, but caught himself just in time.

"See you girls later, then," Rose called over her shoulder to her friends.

He cleared his throat. "Yeah, uh, nice to meet you," he managed to grind out, his voice thick. He dimly registered that Heidi appeared to be smirking, but then they were outside in the freezing air again.

Chapter Nine

He came. He's here, standing in my hometown, just like he said he would be. She stole another look at T.J. from under her lashes. His expression looked almost as dazed as she felt.

He would likely never be called handsome. In fact, the thin sunlight of the winter day made his features look more pronounced — nearly harsh, with his slightly crooked nose, the scar on his cheek that she'd barely noted in the lower lighting when they'd met, and fine grooves around his mouth and eyes. His ears were a bit larger than in her mind's eye, and they looked pink from the cold. He was massive — her memory hadn't exaggerated his enormous height and solid musculature — but his eyes were just as dark and beautiful as she'd recalled. *Just as gorgeous as you've been dreaming that they were*, her inner voice of honesty reminded her.

No, even though he wasn't handsome, he was still the most attractive man she'd ever seen — magnetic, even, at least to her. She loved that he managed to look dangerous and intimidating while he carried their hot chocolates. He'd even apologized to Mr. Gordon, her middle-school geography teacher, who'd been sitting at the table next to theirs at breakfast.

"Would you like to sit here, darlin'?" he asked, his voice the familiar rumbling drawl that she'd feared she might never hear again.

He gestured toward the bench where she'd sat, waiting for him, the day before. Her heart fell, and she made a face.

"No...not there. That's where...well, I was waiting there yesterday," she admitted.

T.J.'s expression was gutted, and it made her feel better. "Oh, honey," he started, but she gently interrupted him.

"I love the benches near the gazebo. They have a view onto the waterfall. It looks like one of them is open, too." She was deliberately focusing on today instead of yesterday, and she could see that T.J. got the heavy-handed hint.

"By all means, darlin'... You lead and I'll follow."

Something about the intensity in his eyes made her think he might be talking about more than just where they would sit. Even after she turned away to look where she was going—she'd prefer not to fall on her face right in front of him, thank you very much—she could still feel his burning gaze on her back. Was he checking out her ass? When she snuck a look back at him, he averted his eyes almost immediately, but it had been obvious for a split second that he'd been ogling her butt. The idea made her feel warm and gooey...or maybe hot and gooey was a better description, given how wildly sexy she found him. He'd brought her the drink she'd mentioned all those months ago, and he couldn't keep his eyes off her. An unwilling excitement blossomed inside her.

When they reached the one sturdy wood-and-metal bench that was unoccupied, he insisted on brushing the small area where a little bit of snow still lingered before he motioned to her to sit down. He sat so close that she could feel the warmth of his body all the way down her side, and his hard thigh felt like a caress against hers as he adjusted his position.

"Your peppermint hot chocolate, ma'am," he drawled. "Complete with candy cane, just the way you said you liked," he finished. She hadn't taken the time to pull on her gloves yet, and his fingers were cold and bare, but the heat when her hand brushed his lightly as she took the cup was undeniable.

"You remembered." She couldn't stop the smile, which she figured probably looked a little moonstruck.

T.J.'s eyes were deep and melting. "I remember everythin' about you, darlin'."

She took a quick, overlarge sip of her cocoa. "Mmm, it's good. Thank you," she answered, deliberately skirting the serious undertones of his statement.

T.J.'s throat worked as he took a swallow of his own drink, and he licked a stray drop from the corner of his mouth. In that moment, she would have given almost anything to be that trace of chocolate.

"Ooh, I *do* like that," he murmured, and for a second, she forgot what they had been talking about. But he continued. "I've never had it like this, so rich. I don't recall that I've ever had anything but the powdered variety," he mused. "What's the peppermint stick for? Flavor?"

"What? How have you missed out on this your whole life?" She didn't have to entirely feign her shock.

T.J. shrugged, and his smile was rueful. "It's a lot hotter where I grew up in Mississippi, and we never had much money for extras like sweets anyway. Then, in the service we did get cocoa occasionally, but only the powdered kind — more stable, I suppose." The brackets next to his mouth deepened as he widened his smile. "This is definitely better. Thank you for tellin' me about it, baby."

Rose flushed with pleasure at being able to introduce T.J. to something he was enjoying. "Oh, wait! You asked about the candy cane... It *is* for flavor," she answered, taking off the lid so she could stir the melting candy into the hot beverage. "But it's also so much better if you sort of nibble off the end then suck the chocolate through the tiny little holes in the peppermint stick." She demonstrated, sucking the hot cocoa up through the minty column of goodness, which intensified the flavor. She'd almost forgotten how small the holes were, though, so she ended up having to suck pretty hard to get much liquid. She chuckled to herself. "Well, that's how we always drank it when we were kids...but that way would probably take me all day, now," she quipped.

When she looked expectantly at T.J., she found that he was staring at her mouth with rapt interest, and his mouth was slightly open. He shifted a little in his seat, and she felt her cheeks heat with awareness.

"Aren't you going to say something?" she asked.

"You're so goddamn beautiful, Rose. I'm sorrier than I can ever say that I left you waitin' yesterday."

His eyes were so earnest that she had to look away, out to the icy waterfall. The river never froze — the water ran too swiftly for that—but in the winter, large pieces of ice would float on the top, making wild splashes and patterns as they went over the edge. The sun was bright enough that the spray from the town's namesake falls made little rainbows.

"I wasn't sure if you changed your mind or if something might have happened...but I understood." She grimaced. "Or, I really tried to," honesty compelled her to add. She turned back toward him. "I know that you have obligations and responsibilities, more urgent and confidential than a lot of other men. You don't have to explain."

"Thank you for that, honey, but I *want* to explain. You deserve that." The quirk of his lips was wry. "Although you're correct that I can't actually say much. But what I *can* tell you is that I was unavoidably detained on assignment, and I was stuck on slow transport, cut off from all comms. It near to broke my heart when I realized I was surely gonna miss our meetin' time and couldn't possibly let you know."

At his words—*"broke my heart"*—Rose's pulse leapt, but T.J. was speaking again.

"I came here to be certain I made things right, if nothin' else. Can you forgive me?" He looked suddenly shy, and if they'd been standing, she would have bet that he would have shuffled his toes. "If...if it even matters to you," he added in a low voice.

"It matters, T.J. I wouldn't have come to meet you yesterday if it didn't matter," she assured him before she could consider her words or stop herself. "But there's nothing to forgive. It's enough that you're here now."

The large grin that spread across his face was radiant, so glorious it felt like it brightened the entire day. No...more than that. She thought he just might have brightened up her life.

T.J. took her free hand into his and made a low sound of dismay. "Aw, honey, your fingers are like ice."

Her entire body tingled as he deftly pulled her whole arm toward his torso, tucking her hand and forearm snugly into the layer of warmth between his sweater and his open coat, so that she could feel every ridge of his hard muscles.

"Oh!" She couldn't help the one small, pleased word, which she exhaled on a cold puff. T.J.'s eyes darkened with unmistakable desire.

"I have mittens." Why did her voice sound so breathy on such mundane statement?

"I like this better," T.J. answered, his voice deep and strained.

"I...do, too," she admitted, biting her lip, aching to close the small distance between them and kiss T.J. with as much passion as she'd been dreaming of for so many months. By some sort of silent, mutual consent, they moved together, but as their lips nearly met, she felt suddenly uncomfortable with how fast things seemed to be moving.

Sure, things had been very intense when they'd met abroad, but those circumstances were unique. There'd been heightened danger, and a very finite timeline before T.J. had to slip away. Now, they were in the middle of the town square and her best friend, middle-school geography teacher, and probably a hundred other people were likely watching her with avid—even if benevolent—interest. She froze.

T.J. seemed to sense the change in her and immediately backed off. "I'm sorry, honey. I must've misread you, there." His laugh was self-deprecating.

"This isn't goin' a'tall the way I imagined it…dreamed about it." A dull red stained his prominent cheekbones, and she'd noticed previously that his accent seemed to get more pronounced when he felt nervous. "You might be embarrassed to be seen with a brute like me. It wouldn't be the first time… I don't blame you. It was darker when we met."

"No, no…you didn't misread me," she hurried to reassure him. "And I like the way you look…*really* like it. You're so…tough and sexy." She rushed to continue when she realized how much she'd revealed. "It's only…it's been so many months, and…it doesn't really matter, but I'm pretty sure I can feel about half of the town staring at us right now."

As she spoke, some of the tension drained out of T.J.'s frame, which she could both see and feel, given their close proximity.

"I understand completely, darlin'. It's been a while, but my own hometown is pretty small, too. Most days I'd swear it runs purely on gossip and fried catfish." He stroked his thumb along the back of her hand where their clasped fingers were hidden under his coat, and the sensuality of the gesture made another visible breath escape her lips in a round puff.

"How 'bout we spend today the way you described all those months ago, in my arms? You can show me around this charmin' town?" T.J.'s words were innocent enough, but the gravelly undertone of them was suggestive. She understood what he was doing, though. He was proposing something that would give them a chance to get more comfortable with one another again. Before she could overthink it, she blurted out her answer.

"I'd love that." As she spoke, she realized that she really would. Buoyed by excitement, the air seemed fresher, the sun warmer, everything about the day bright and shiny again.

"It's a date, then." He drew out the words like molasses, winking at her so that she giggled.

"Tough and sexy, *hm*?" he added. The grin he shot her was cocky as they rose, and he offered her his arm. She felt her face heat all the way up to the roots of her hair.

Chapter Ten

Guiding T.J. around downtown Hunt's Falls on Christmas Eve made Rose fall in love with her hometown all over again, and she could practically feel her granny's spirit walking along with them. They started by making a full circuit of all the storefronts, T.J. keeping Rose's arm tucked securely in his, except for a few times where it got a bit more crowded so that he pulled her under his shoulder. She felt cherished and protected, just as she had when they'd first met, but here, it was sweeter. *Maybe because I can just enjoy the moment*, she realized. They didn't need to worry about danger or secrets...but could simply enjoy each other, surrounded by the joyful spirit of the town and season.

As they stopped in front of another detailed display, this one a sort of imaginary North Pole carnival, complete with Santa and the reindeer riding a double-wheel Ferris wheel, T.J.'s low whistle was impressed.

"This one is definitely my favorite," Rose enthused.

He chuckled. "That's what you said about the last three, darlin'."

"Well, they're all so awesome…and I can't get over how detailed they are. Some of the older shops have been using the same displays for a long time, and those are totally classic, but so many are new and creative, too."

T.J. nodded. "The workmanship is impressive. Can you imagine how fiddly it would be to put in hundreds of teeny-tiny screws into somethin' like that?" He gestured toward one of the miniature mechanical rides. "As someone who has been involved in a lot of unusual building projects over the course of my career, I applaud their patience."

She eyed him with curiosity. "Are you… Can you talk about anything that you've done? Or are you only allowed to give me your name, rank and serial number?"

The twist of T.J.'s lips was rueful. "I can give you a little beyond that, but not much. You probably already know more than you ought to." He paused. "It's Lieutenant Colonel Timothy Jefferson Browning, and I enlisted in the United States Marine Corps over twenty years ago now."

"Twenty years?" she asked, genuinely surprised. She'd known he was older, but that was a long time.

"Joined up as soon as I turned eighteen, partly to get away, but also because I wanted to start sendin' money home to take care of my little sister." He paused, and she had the impression that he was debating whether he should say anything more. Something must have tipped the scales, though, because he continued. "My momma and stepdaddy were both… Well, let's just say they weren't great at caregivin'. My stepdaddy wasn't good at much of anythin' else, for that matter, although my momma did try her best to love us, in her way."

His dark eyes flashed, looking curiously vulnerable. "And now you know that I come by most of my rough looks naturally, and I'm probably too old for you." His laugh had a bitter edge. "Definitely worn around the edges."

She leaned into the warm, hardness of his body, lifting up on her tiptoes to kiss his cheek, which was slightly scratchy. "Doesn't change a thing for me," she whispered. "As someone raised mostly by a single grandmother and now a trauma nurse, please believe that I have my own worn edges, even if you can't see them," she added. He squeezed her to him, just for an instant, but it was enough.

They both turned back to the window, and T.J. took a deep breath.

"What is that smell?" he asked. "It's…"

"Incredible?" she suggested. "Enticing?"

"I mean, not as enticing as you…but it's up there," he agreed, making her blush at his husky undertone.

"It's the nut roaster. He must be back in the square. I thought you'd like to try them. I even got you some yesterday but I, um, ate them all last night," Rose finished lamely, remembering devouring them over the lump in her throat through champagne-induced tears.

"Well, then, we should definitely get a new bag…or three," T.J. answered, waggling his eyebrows to make her smile again.

Fifteen minutes later, they'd settled down on another bench with several warm, red-and-white-striped bags, since T.J. had insisted on buying every single type she'd suggested. He put his arm around her easily, and she scooted closer to him so they were nearly cuddled together. She knew it was skirting the bounds of potential PDA, especially for staid Hunt's Falls. She just didn't want to be any farther away from him than she had to be, and he'd made it clear with constant small touches that he felt the same way. When T.J. popped the first roasted nut into his mouth, he made a deep sound of pleasure so sensual that she felt her nipples tighten and her core go liquid.

"Oh, hell, these taste even better than they smell," he said with a groan. "You have to try one." Before she realized his intent, he slid a warm, caramelized-sugar-salted-crust-covered morsel into her mouth, brushing her lips with his hard fingertips with exquisite gentleness so that she shivered at the sensation.

"Cold, honey?" he asked, pulling her closer until she was nearly on his lap.

I want to be on his lap, a naughty voice whispered in her mind. *Even better if we were alone and both naked.* She nearly shivered again before she forced the stray thoughts away and savored the treat T.J. had fed her.

"We can go somewhere inside," he continued in a worried tone, and Rose realized she'd never answered him.

"No, no...I'm fine. I'm not ready to go inside yet," she answered, and her unspoken words hung between them. She wanted to stay exactly where she was, with T.J.

They both turned their attention to the massive Christmas tree in front of them, which stretched so high it seemed like it ended in the brilliant blue of the sky. Since none of the buildings downtown were taller than two stories, the only other structures of a similar height were several church steeples.

"That is an incredible tree," T.J. observed. "I don't know that I've ever seen anything like it."

Rose turned toward him in surprise. "Really? What about the town where you grew up?"

He shrugged. "We didn't have a town tree — or not that I can remember. We had a whole lot of swampland and gators...although the mangroves *are* pretty, draped in Spanish moss. You'll get chiggers if you touch 'em, though. I've seen people hang lights on them from time to time, even though I've never had that particular inclination."

"What about other places you've spent Christmas?" she asked.

He looked thoughtful as he sampled a few more nuts. "Well, in my line of work, we don't often get time off for the holidays — and even if there is a choice, they're always lookin' for volunteers who don't mind workin'. I suppose that I don't have the best memories from more recent times, either, although I did get to spend some time with my sister and her family a year or so ago."

Rose found the idea of him volunteering to work over Christmas every year so others could be with their families deeply kind...considerate in the way she was coming to understand was just part of T.J.'s makeup.

He shifted next to her, rubbing their thighs together, but she got the sense that his movement was almost sheepish.

"I, ah, don't know if I should feel badly about it, but I just realized I never mentioned that I was engaged before. She and I never spent a full Christmas together, though. Just abbreviated ones... I tended to get called away a lot. It caused some tension...but then, almost everything did with my ex, at least at the end. It's nearly two years ago now."

Rose wondered if she should be upset, but no matter how she considered it, she found that she really...wasn't. "You shouldn't feel badly. We both had lives before we met."

"That's quite progressive of you, Ms. Abbott. I'm guessin' you left a long line of disappointed beaus behind you."

The snort that escaped before she could stop it wasn't very dignified, and her hand flew to cover her mouth.

"Hit a nerve, did I?" T.J. teased.

"I wouldn't call it a long line, no... I never really got serious with anyone, although I suppose part of that is because I kept them at a distance. Then they always proved me right by breaking up with me," she admitted.

She didn't know why T.J.'s possessive snarl caused delicious goosebumps to rise all over her skin, but it totally did.

"I don't like imaginin' you with anyone else, baby, but if they were dumb enough to let you walk away, I pity them." His voice was dark and harsh, and she thought the tightening of his arm was likely unintentional. Her stomach felt like it did a little flip of excitement.

"I think your ex-fiancée was an idiot, too," she breathed, surprising a bark of laughter from T.J.

A jingling sound near their bench made them both turn toward it. Rose felt a flare of excitement at seeing a horse-drawn carriage, all decked out in Christmas finery, complete with red ribbons and pine garlands. The horses' breath puffed white in the cold air, and the vehicle slowed to a stop at the end of the block, in front of a hand-lettered sign she'd somehow missed before. It read, *'Carriage Rides Upon Request'*. It was as if her mind had conjured it from thin air, to make today the date of her dreams.

When she realized she was staring at the horses like a little girl in the first flush of princess-obsession, she forced her gaze away. *It's totally fine if we don't take a ride,* she told herself. *T.J. might not like carriages or horses. It might already be booked.*

T.J. took one look at her face and jumped to his feet.

"I'll be right back, darlin'," he promised, and his determined expression warmed her from the inside out.

"It's okay if we can't go," she answered, wanting to be sure that he knew she wouldn't be disappointed.

"Let me see what I can do." His voice sounded as ominous as the grim lines of his face appeared, and she had the sudden memory of the way he'd looked when the man had dragged her out of the cave. T.J. was every inch the relentless Marine, and she wasn't going to get in his way...especially not when his goal was to do something for her. She nodded.

T.J. stalked over to the older driver, intending to do whatever he needed to ensure that he and Rose got to take a Christmas Eve carriage ride. He cursed himself for not bringing more cash, and he let his face slip into the familiar harsh lines of battle. Instead, in the end, it was shockingly easy. The man, who looked a bit like a Norwegian Santa Claus, with his Scandinavian sweater stretched over his rounded stomach and medium-length white beard — albeit a neatly trimmed one — confirmed that he was available for the next forty-five minutes or so and would be happy to take the two of them. T.J. surreptitiously paid him, adding a healthy tip. It was Christmas Eve, after all, but T.J. also hoped the extra gratuity might convince the driver to look the other way if he and Rose snuck in a few kisses along the ride, since it seemed like that might be considered slightly scandalous behavior around here. T.J.'s heart thumped harder in his chest at the idea, and he wondered when he'd last been so excited about a woman's lips. He'd missed her taste so much, though. *Maybe I can even touch her, under the blanket.* With that thought, he nearly had to adjust his pants, which had become suddenly too tight...again.

When he returned to where she waited for him on the bench, her face lit up so brightly it stole his breath, and he thought he would have done just about anything to bring that expression to her face every day.

"You did it?" she asked, clutching the packages of nuts, now folded again, to her chest.

"It's all ours for the next forty-five minutes," he confirmed.

"Oh, T.J.!" She beamed, and he thought that if her hands hadn't been full, she might have clapped. He couldn't stop the wide grin that spread over his face. If his brothers from his unit could see him now, they'd hardly recognize him...then tease him mercilessly for how soft his Rose made him. Right now, he would have taken the razzing gladly...*proudly*, even.

When they got to the carriage, Rose greeted the driver warmly, calling him Mr. Donovan—*and does everyone really know everyone else in this town?*—then cooed at the horses. "What are their names?" she asked.

The older man's—Mr. Donovan's—faded blue eyes twinkled. "Why, Rudolph and Dominick, of course."

Now that T.J. had taken the bags from her, this time Rose did clap delightedly. Looking at her, with the tree and snowy town square behind her, her gray-blue eyes shining, her spun-gold hair tousled around her face and shoulders, and her nose and cheeks rosy from the cold, he didn't think he'd ever seen anything so lovely. *Now I'm becoming a damn poet*, he grumbled to himself, but the thought didn't dim his mood in the slightest. He'd found her, she'd forgiven him, and they were going to take the carriage ride of her dreams.

T.J. helped her into the carriage, glaring at Mr. Donovan when he made a move to assist. T.J. certainly didn't need any help climbing in, and if he had his way, nobody else would ever touch Rose again. The older man backed off instantly with a gleam of understanding in his knowing gaze.

Instead, he just passed them two thick blankets. "It can get cold on the longer rides especially, since we like to go out on the dirt roads at the edge of town. Breeze picks up there."

T.J. put his arm around Rose's shoulders, pulling her tightly against him so their bodies pressed together — and he didn't think the thrill of feeling her so close would ever lessen — before draping the blankets over their laps and tucking them in on the sides. As he shifted, his head brushed against Rose's cheek.

"Oh, T.J., your ears must be freezing!" she exclaimed, concern heavy in her voice. "Will you be too cold? Maybe you can wrap my scarf around your head."

His answering scowl was so dark he was surprised his face didn't crack. "I would *never* take your scarf. I want you to be warm and toasty, darlin'. Don't worry about me a bit. Believe me, I've dealt with worse." Much, much worse in fact, but he wouldn't have gone into details with her, even if he could. He'd nearly lost three toes to frostbite on one op.

Mr. Donovan cleared his throat. "I, ah, always bring along some extra caps, in case people get cold while we're out there. June over at that Juniper's Knotty Knits shop makes them, and people like to buy them as souvenirs this time of year."

"Oh, that's perfect!" Rose enthused. T.J. was a little bit more skeptical — *what the heck kind of cheesy keepsake hat could it be?* — but he was willing to do anything not to spoil this for Rose. He passed over the reasonable amount Mr. Donovan had named without hesitation. What the older man took out of the bag next to him, though, was even more unexpected. It was a hand-knit, cherry-red Santa hat, with an enormous pouf and little silver sleigh bell on the top tip.

Rose's peal of laughter was like a handbell, clear and sweet. "Well, that's...unexpected." She giggled.

"Don't think I can pull it off?" he teased, and he could tell he'd surprised her.

"I mean, it's a bit hard to picture." She cocked her head to one side as if imagining it, her eyes crinkling at the corners with mirth.

Determinedly, he took the cap from Mr. Donovan with a mumbled thank-you, then shoved it onto his head. The warmth was instant — and damn if it wasn't the most comfortable hat he'd ever worn.

He expected Rose to giggle again, but instead, she hugged his massive arm tightly to her, and her eyes were shining suspiciously.

"You're wonderful," she whispered, leaning closer so that her next words were directly into his ear. "And you look so sexy in that hat, being silly just for me, that I am barely stopping myself from tearing your clothes off."

His mouth was still open when they pulled away from the curb with a merry jingle.

Chapter Eleven

Magical was the only word to describe the ride. They clip-clopped through town, going by all the major town landmarks — few as they were — before steering past the Victorian mansions, then beyond the edge of the town limits to the surrounding cornfields. Mr. Donovan, who Rose remembered as the owner of the local hardware store before he'd retired and his son had taken over, made the occasional clicking noise to the horses, but was otherwise silent. She snuggled into T.J.'s side, inhaling his scent — the one that had haunted her reveries — of soap and something masculine and spicy, now combined with the leather smell of his jacket.

When they passed by the frozen pond at the edge of the town nature preserve, it looked so picturesque that she sighed with pleasure. "Oh, isn't that beautiful?" she asked, admiring the view.

"Stunnin'," T.J. agreed, but when she turned toward him, he was looking at her instead of the ice and forest. She felt her cheeks heat.

"You're outrageous." She tried to tease him, but her voice came out husky instead.

"I am," he agreed easily. "At least when it comes to you, darlin'." His eyes darkened. "Can I confess somethin', pretty Rose?"

She nodded, holding his gaze wordlessly as she felt the brisk breeze tugging at her hair.

"Leavin' you alone in that cave might have been the hardest thing I've ever done, and not a day has gone by that I haven't thought of you, wishin' I could see you, hold you like this." His voice was low, but the intensity of his words — and the emotion behind them — made every nerve ending in her body take notice.

"I thought of you, too," she confessed. "Every day. Every night, I wanted you with me, even though I told myself I was crazy after only knowing you such a short time."

He gave a strangled groan and squeezed her shoulders. "If you're crazy, so am I."

She thrilled at his admission. "Did…did you send me messages?"

T.J.'s smile was crooked, almost sheepish. "Yeah… work's been nonstop for months now, with constant restrictions, and I really shouldn't have sent anythin'… but I hoped you'd understand."

It warmed her all over again, having the proof of his messages that he'd been thinking of her when they were apart. "I missed you, but of course I understood. It's not quite the same, but I'm used to my brother being out of touch for weeks or months at a time."

"That's how it's been my whole career, and I've always been proud of what I do, servin' without hesitation, but…for the first time, I didn't *want* to be away. I wished I could have come to you sooner." His tone was harsh, intense, and she shivered with awareness and…something more.

"T.J.," she breathed, then his mouth was on hers and the rest of the world fell away. His taste was just as she remembered, only now with the faint addition of mint and chocolate, and he devoured her as if he never wanted to let her go. Her heart beat double-time, and suddenly she couldn't seem to get close enough to him, even as he stroked his tongue into her mouth, caressing, and crushed her against him so that the blanket crumpled between them. When at last they separated, she could hear her own panting, along with the steady hoofbeats of the horses, combined with the jingling bridle.

Mr. Donovan was so careful not to even remotely turn his head that she knew he must have seen or heard them…or both. She should have been scandalized, but she found that she felt too content in T.J.'s arms to care.

When she looked up at his face, his lips were slightly swollen from their kisses, and his cheeks were extra red, not just from the chill. He averted his eyes at first, then met her gaze head-on, remorse filling his.

"So sorry, baby. I, ah, I'm afraid I got carried away for a moment." The apology sounded sincere, although not exactly regretful.

Leaning in so close that her lips actually brushed his earlobe, making him shudder, she whispered her answer. "Don't be. I'm not sorry at all, and I hope you do it again soon…although maybe more privately."

His dark eyes flashed surprise, then unmistakable interest and something more tender, too. "You can count on it," he vowed, moving his hand under the blanket that covered their laps until he was almost stroking right over her mound. She felt the touch as if it were electric, even through their clothing. When she gasped, stifling the sound almost immediately, his answering grin was wolfish, but he moved his hand lower to squeeze her thigh instead.

As the carriage swayed, she felt every tiny motion as if it were a stroke of his hand or body against hers, and it ratcheted up her desire until she thought she might scream as they made one final tour around downtown.

Before she knew it, she was standing on the brick walkway of the town square again, her arm tucked back in T.J.'s. Unconsciously, she swayed toward him. As the carriage drove off—with Mr. Donovan shooting them a kindly look over his shoulder as he wished them one last '*Merry Christmas*'—Rose longed to be alone with T.J. so badly it was like an ache in her chest.

"Darlin'," T.J. said, making her shiver at how low and rough his voice sounded. "I was feelin' optimistic earlier—or preparin' for the worst, dependin' on how you look at it—and called the Victorian inn around the corner. They had a last-minute cancellation, so I booked their last room. Would you like to come with me and, ah, warm up?"

He was such an endearing mixture of possessive confidence about his work, and sweet shyness about his own appeal, that her heart wanted to melt into a puddle…even while the undertone of his words made her thrill.

"If '*warm up*' is code for you kissing me again—everywhere—then absolutely," she answered, giving a startled yelp when he grabbed her and swung her easily into a bridal carry.

"T.J.!" she laughed. "I'm too heavy! What are you doing? Put me down!" She batted at his shoulder, but it was like swatting a marble sculpture. He took big strides toward the inn, which she'd always secretly loved for its old-fashioned style, a throw-back to the early days of Hunt's Falls. Beyond not appearing to strain under her weight, he didn't even seem to be getting winded, and she remembered how easily he'd carried her before when they'd first met.

"I'm not givin' you a chance to change your mind," he answered, and she wasn't entirely sure he was joking.

"I'm not going to change my mind," she answered, giving in to her impulse to tuck her head against his neck and inhale. He smelled like leather and spice, and a tiny bit sweaty. She loved it.

They walked by a family on the sidewalk, and one of the kids openly gawked at her, looking concerned.

"It's okay," T.J. assured the little girl. "She just twisted her ankle," he lied, and the little girl nodded understandingly. The rest of the family looked mollified, too. Rose felt her cheeks go hot.

"You're *incorrigible*," she hissed as soon as they were out of earshot.

He grinned unrepentantly. "I still get to hold you, though, don't I?" he returned.

T.J. knew he should put Rose down, especially when they entered the cinnamon-scented lobby of the Victorian inn, which was decked out to the nines, with every single corner stuffed full of holiday knick-knacks. Now that he had her back in his arms, though, he just couldn't seem to release her. It felt like she'd always been meant to be there.

As he strode toward the dark-wood desk, the matronly clerk looked slightly alarmed.

"T.J. Browning checking in. I called earlier for a reservation," he said as soon as they got close enough for her to hear him.

"Oh, yes, of course. The Honeymoon Suite…but we call it the Santa Suite this time of year. I have everything ready here." She looked relieved that he was a guest, at least, and pushed an envelope toward him. Her gray curls were fluffy around her face and waved a bit as she craned her neck to try to look at Rose's face. "Is…is everything all right, dear?" she asked.

"Yes, I'm fine, Mrs. Henderson…no worries," Rose reassured her, blushing furiously as she grabbed the check-in package. *Rose might have moved away from Hunt's Falls*, he mused, *but everyone seems to remember her as if she'd never left.*

Some imp of mischief made T.J. lean in closer as he answered. "It's only that I just got off several month's deployment, so I can't stand to put her down," he confided, enjoying the indignant squawk from Rose more than he should.

The older woman's dark eyes widened, then grew wistful. She looked suddenly younger, and her cheeks pinkened. "Well, now, isn't that lovely? My Frank was always the same when he got back, too." Her faraway gaze was obviously seeing something from her past that made her smile. "We have a special Christmas Eve menu tonight, but we also offer it as room service to certain suites, including yours, just so you're aware. Your key is in the envelope, and the signs are easy to follow once you reach the second floor. Don't let me keep you." Her smile was such a delightful combination of grandmotherly and indulgent that he had to chuckle as they walked away.

"That woman was my Sunday school teacher!" Rose whispered, sounding scandalized as he walked her up the grand staircase. "Her husband used to brag about her caramel apple crumble at nearly every potluck."

"Sounds like a very happy marriage, indeed," he answered, raising his eyebrows suggestively. Rose's snort turned into a giggle.

According to the signs, their room should be just ahead, but T.J. couldn't read the brass plate on the large door because it was obscured by a giant wreath. "Darlin', can you get the key out for me?" he asked Rose. "My hands are a bit full at the moment."

For a second, she looked like she might argue, but instead surprised him by pulling out the old-fashioned metal key and putting it into the lock, tacitly agreeing to let him carry her over the threshold. When he entered, he was so surprised that he paused just inside the door, only vaguely hearing it close behind him. The room was incredible...massive, with an enormous four-poster bed, balcony and palatial clawfoot tub, but what made it even more stunning was the fully decorated Victorian Christmas tree in the corner, along with the opulent dining table set for two.

When he looked down at Rose, her mouth had dropped open with wonder. "Oh, T.J.! This is amazing!" The way her eyes sparkled did something to his gut. "But...isn't it too much?" She bit her lower lip, and he longed to kiss it better.

"Don't worry, honey. *Nothin'* is too much for you, but if it makes you feel any better, they were so happy to get someone last-minute on Christmas Eve that I don't know if they're chargin' me half what it must be worth." Looking around, he realized that this was exactly the kind of set-up he'd dreamed of as a kid but had never gotten to experience. "My God, if my younger self could see me now, he'd think all his dreams had come true." He spoke without thinking, but he couldn't regret the words, even though it normally made him deeply uncomfortable to talk about how he grew up, so often hungry and afraid.

"*All* his dreams?" she asked softly, touching his face in a way that made him ache.

"Well, I'm carryin' the most beautiful woman I've ever laid eyes on over to a huge bed, and she's lookin' at me like she loves bein' alone with me...so yeah, pretty much. Younger T.J. had a bit of a one-track mind." His smile was self-deprecating.

"I like the way he thinks," she teased, then her smile turned sultry. "And that we're on our way to the bed."

Any other thoughts fled from T.J.'s mind at her words, and he carried her over to the sleeping area, noting with satisfaction that the mattress had to be a king or California king. He laid her onto it and stretched out next to her with such alacrity that she laughed.

"You wild man! We still have our boots and coats on!" she protested.

He leaped to his feet again, quickly tearing off his offending footwear and jacket. "Easy fix," he proclaimed, raising both of his eyebrows, then pulled her boots off as well and helped her shrug out of her outer things and coat. When he reclined next to her again, he could see from the rapid rise and fall of her chest that she was breathless, and he felt curiously winded as well...anticipating. He wanted to hug her, touch her, stroke her...but he also felt almost shy.

The face she turned toward him was slightly bashful, too, until she moved her gaze to his hairline and her expression transformed to one of mirth. "You still have your Santa hat on!" she said.

"Well, now, isn't that interestin'? Wanna come sit on my lap, baby girl, and tell me what you want for Christmas?" he drawled, giving her a mock leer. He was teasing, but when her breathing quickened further at his words, he sat up on the bed and pulled her, squealing, onto his lap.

She laughed, wiggling. Her little gasp revealed the moment she had to have felt his rising hardness below her.

"Have you been naughty or nice?" he asked, his voice gravelly with sudden need.

Rose's expression was playful, but her eyes were hot with desire that matched his own. "Well, I tried to be nice, but sometimes I missed you so much..."

A jealous beast roared to vicious life inside of him. "You... Was there someone else?" The words came out strangled, even as he hated himself for asking.

The shock on her face was total, and he knew it was unfeigned. "*What?* No! We... I thought... Wait! Has there been someone else for *you*? It *has* been a long time."

He was almost offended she would ask, but he had started the line of questioning. "Absolutely not, darlin'. I didn't want anyone but you...was only dreamin' of seein' you again."

She looked a bit huffy as she resettled herself on his lap, like a cat with its fur all ruffled. He wanted to stroke her back, but he was smart enough to know that he'd better hold off a moment. He narrowed his eyes as he thought about what she'd said.

"Wait. So what did you mean...?" he paused, the pieces clicking together. "Oh...*oh!*"

Rose blushed and stiffened. "I was trying to be sexy...and apparently failing pretty freaking hard."

She would have gotten off his lap, but he held her there. "You were extremely sexy. I'm the one who was bein' an insecure idiot. I'm sorry, baby. I suppose I'm just, well, not used to women choosin' me, because I grew up so poor that I was always considered trash — and on account of my looks." He sighed, loosening his arms. "I'm sorry. Don't feel like you have to stay," he forced himself to say.

Rose touched his cheek so he looked up at her, and her expression didn't seem angry. In fact, she looked tender...even if a little uncertain. He hated that he'd caused her to doubt him, even for a moment.

"Do you still *want* me to stay here?" she asked, and those slate-blue eyes of hers that had been getting him through every shitty mission just lately held vulnerability.

"God, yes, I want you here," he admitted. "More than anythin'."

"Well, good, because I like where I am," she answered, shifting her hips so that he hardened underneath her all over again, and he groaned.

"Rose, honey, you couldn't be more perfect for me...but you are *definitely* goin' on the naughty list."

Her sparkling laughter made everything inside of him ease. As naturally as breathing, he shifted their positions so he was on top of her and covered her mouth with his.

Chapter Twelve

Often over the last few months and most particularly at night — when he had any time to sleep — just before he drifted off, T.J. had imagined what it might be like to have Rose underneath him in a bed instead of on the hard cave floor. The sensation in real life exceeded his wildest imaginings, and he thrilled at the unique taste and feel of her that no amount of time or distance had been able to erase from his memory. She was soft and eager, opening her mouth to him so he could stroke his tongue along hers, even as she opened her thighs as well so that his hardness settled against her core, hot even through the layers of their clothes.

He caressed her everywhere he could reach, brushing her hair away from her face and rolling them slightly so all his weight was no longer on top of her, allowing his hands to roam more freely. He nibbled at her full bottom lip as he ran one hand down her back to cup her lush ass while he tucked his other hand just underneath her sweater to touch the bare skin of her lower back. She moaned against his lips, arching herself closer so that the fullness of her breasts was pressed against his chest. He sucked in a harsh breath.

"Dreamed about this so many times," he murmured, only half-conscious of what he was saying. He didn't regret it, though, especially when she answered.

"Me, too, T.J. You feel so good." She punctuated her words by taking control of the kiss, nipping at his lower lip. She was demanding, and he loved it.

"Tryin' to tell me somethin', darlin'?" His voice was husky, deep, and she shivered.

"Want you to touch me…kiss me…everywhere," she panted, clutching him to her as though she wanted to have her hands all over him at once.

At her words and her desperate tone, his cock thickened and swelled until he thought he might just shoot off in his jeans. He wanted to tear both of their clothes off and surge into her like a beast, but he forced himself to slow down. His Rose deserved everything she'd ever wanted, and if she desired more touches, he was happy to oblige. Still, his hands shook as he gently pulled off her sweater and jeans, caressing her skin everywhere in the process, until she wore only baby-pink cotton panties and a matching bra.

"Touch and kiss you everywhere, hmm?" he rumbled, barely recognizing his own voice before he lowered his head to her neck, kissing a trail down her chest as he lowered the cups of her bra. The round bounty of her breasts tumbled out, tipped by the hardened points of her pink nipples, and he didn't know if he'd ever seen anything more beautiful.

When he pulled one taut nipple into his mouth, she hummed and tightened her grip. As he licked and sucked, swirling his tongue around the tip, the little gasping, incoherent noises she made ratcheted up his arousal to a fever pitch. He released her with an audible pop, switching to the other side, even as he snaked his hand between them to cup her mound. She was hot and wet, even through the thin barrier of her underwear. By shifting her hips, she put herself more firmly into his hand in a wordless invitation, and lust surged inside of his chest. He pushed the fabric to the side so he could stroke two questing fingers into her folds and found her drenched with cream.

"You're so wet for me, baby," he marveled, his voice muffled by the nub he was still teasing. Her answer was a whimper, and she rotated her hips jerkily as he traced her clit with the lightest of pressure.

"Oh my God," she whispered in a harsh, needy puff.

A wild masculine satisfaction filled him as he realized she was already close to reaching her peak, and he redoubled his efforts at her breast and with measured, gentle strokes until she tightened against him with a long wail, her pussy going even slicker with a surge of honey. He drew out her pleasure for as long as he could, reveling in her shudders, until she was relaxed and sweaty against him. Feeling inordinately proud but also wildly turned on, he brought his hand to his mouth, licking her musky, tangy flavor from his fingers. Rose watched him with shocked eyes, but they were also filled with arousal.

"So fuckin' beautiful, Rose, and delicious... Been wantin' to taste you again for so goddamn long." He shifted so he caged her in with his arms and legs. She looked thoroughly ravished, with pink marks of his possession on her neck and breasts, but he wanted more. So much more. "Tell me you'll let me taste your pussy again, right from the source."

Her cheeks colored delightfully, and he loved that his Rose was still shy.

"I...ah, if you want to," she stammered, even as the hard little points of her nipples practically taunted him with her arousal.

"More than anythin'," he answered, his voice going hoarse with desire. No, it was beyond desire...desperation. He didn't know if he'd ever wanted anything more than he wanted Rose — every part of her — in that moment.

He reached around to unhook her bra, throwing it somewhere — he didn't honestly care if it sailed into the fire — before he slid her panties down her legs almost reverently and settled between them on his stomach.

"Put your arms up, baby, and hold on to the post," he growled, and he saw goosebumps rise on her skin. He'd noticed before that his woman liked it when he was bossy, and he intended to take full advantage of that since he fucking loved being in charge with her.

She did as he'd asked — *ordered* — and the movement and position thrust her full breasts forward so that they shook and wobbled. He couldn't hold back his feral snarl before he bent his head to lap at her core.

Her taste from his fingers had been just as delicious as he remembered, but direct from the source, it was unbelievable. He licked her from the bottom to the top of her slit, determined to taste every last drop, before focusing on the bundle of nerves that made her squirm and thrash underneath him. Still, even though he could tell she wanted to move, she never let go of the bedpost behind her, even as she tightened her thighs around his ears in a convulsive motion.

When he pushed first one thick finger, then a second into her sheath, curving them upward as he continued his sensual onslaught, her high-pitched cries took on a more urgent tone.

"Oh...oh, T.J.," she moaned, pushing her hips up helplessly to meet his every lick and stroke. "I think I'm going to..." She broke off with a gasp.

"That's it, darlin'. Come again for your man. Show me that you're mine," he ordered, his face still pressed against her pussy. When he swirled his tongue around the button of her pleasure, he felt her stiffen, her back bowing until she might have fallen off the bed if she hadn't been holding on. Her channel tightened around his fingers, and she gave a broken cry before she collapsed, shuddering, underneath him. He continued licking her and stroking lazily into her until she was only trembling a little. From his vantage point, between her soft thighs, she looked nearly drunk on pleasure, and he fought the inappropriate urge to beat his chest with primal satisfaction. *He'd* done that. T.J. Browning, the good-for-nothing, ugly poor kid from the Mississippi bayou, had made an angel scream with ecstasy.

"Oh, T.J.," she sighed, and he crawled up the bed to take her into his arms again.

T.J. was an amazing lover. *No,* Rose mentally amended. *He's* better *than amazing. He's spectacular, and he hasn't even been inside me yet.* Rose's smile dimmed at the realization that, for the third time, T.J. had brought her immense satisfaction but showed no signs of wanting to fully make love to her. She knew he was hard and turned on. She'd felt his monster erection against her core earlier.

"Satisfied, darlin'?" he drawled, tracing his fingers along her spine so that she shivered. Or maybe it was his sexy voice that was making her so crazy.

"So satisfied I'm not sure there are any bones left in my body," she answered honestly, but hesitated to say anything more. Still, he must have heard something in her voice.

"But?" he prompted. When she still held back, he spoke again. "You can tell me anythin', Rose."

On an elemental level, she believed that…knew it, to the marrow of her bones. She trusted T.J. with her body, and she thought she might be coming to trust him with her heart. She could trust him enough to speak openly. She took a deep breath.

"Don't you…want me to touch you? Or to, um, make love to me?" She spoke all in a rush, intent on getting the words out, but he seemed to understand. "You never, uh, you know…in the cave, either."

His rough fingertip on her cheek felt intimate as he guided her to look into his eyes, and the tenderness she could read in them made her melt all over again.

"I want that…*so much*, baby. But I also want more with you." His gaze was searching. "I don't want you to feel that this is only physical for me. You deserve everythin'…the world itself." His small smile was crooked. "You could do so much better than me."

Her heart felt like it flipped over in her chest, and she wanted to both kiss him silly and shake him. "I may not be very experienced, but I know the difference between attraction and true caring…and I felt something deeper for you almost as soon as we met."

T.J. quirked his lips up. "Was that before or after you threatened to stab me?"

She snorted. "Well, actually, it might have been because you understood that I had to protect myself, and you didn't judge me for it. Instead, you treated me with respect." Saying it out loud, she realized it was true. Even knowing that she was physically no match for him, T.J. had always treated her like an equal.

"I wanted you then, and I want you even more now," she admitted, her voice husky with feeling. "But you got one thing wrong."

He raised his eyebrows, his fingers tracing along the curve of her face with exquisite gentleness. "What's that, darlin'?"

"There is *nobody* better than you—not for me," she answered, with feeling. The expressions that flitted across his face in rapid succession were a combination of hesitation, hope and dark desire, before he crushed her to him again.

As T.J. slanted his mouth over hers, devouring her, she reveled in the sensation of her naked skin against the textures of his sweater and jeans. Something about the contrast made her feel wild and wanton, like her inner temptress had free rein. He smelled spicy and warm, safe and exciting all at once, and she inhaled deeply, wanting to draw as much of him into her lungs as she could.

"I was plannin' to be a gentleman, but when you say things like that, I don't know if I can," he rumbled, his voice vibrating against her neck before he nipped her lightly, making her tremble with need.

"Don't be, then. Just be yourself," she answered, trailing her nails lightly over his short hair as she peppered his face with kisses.

"Ah, God, Rose...*Rose*." He repeated her name tenderly, over and over, as his hands seemed like they were everywhere at once. Then, suddenly, he was standing next to the bed, tearing off his clothes faster than she'd ever seen anyone get undressed.

Her eyes widened with each body part he uncovered until he stood with the outline of his impressive nude form highlighted by the changing light of the late-afternoon sunset. He looked like a warrior of old, his muscles strong and defined, covered with scars that ranged from small to large, angry red to faded and shiny. His expression was complex, filled with both intense need and yearning. When she followed the trail of dark hair from his chest down to his groin, his cock stood, massive and red, twitching and leaking a drop of moisture, even as she stared at it.

Rose gulped. "You're...huge," she whispered. Her channel clenched, even as she worried that he might not fit inside her after all.

Instantly, her fierce warlord transformed into her tender lover. "I can go real slow, honey, and make sure you love every second...every inch. But we could also save this for another day."

A wave of affection...and probably a lot more than affection...broke over her at the combination of agony and stoic resignation she saw in his eyes. T.J. was showing her that he put her first, and she realized that she loved him for it. She loved him, period.

"No...I, ah, I want you inside me," she breathed, feeling her nipples tighten and her sex pulsed in anticipation. "But, um, slow sounds good," she admitted.

T.J.'s grin was wolfish, but then he froze. "Aw...*fuck*," he said.

She felt her stomach flip. He'd changed his mind. He had some horrible secret. He had to leave, immediately.

The possibilities raced through her head. "What?" she said, fearing it was more of a croak than a word.

The dark red color she'd seen before tinted his cheeks, and he rubbed the back of his neck uncomfortably. "I brought condoms, just in case, but, uh, they're in my bag, in my car." He moved as if to put his pants back on, but held out one hand as if to hold her where she was. "Don't move a single inch, baby. Stay just like that while I'm gone, or if you want to, go ahead and pet that pretty pussy so it'll be nice and wet when I get back."

Her lips parted on a silent exhale of shocked arousal, and she flexed her hips. The naughty part of her brain took over and she let her thighs fall open, just a little, to show T.J. how wet she still was from their earlier play. It touched her that he would stop and run out to his car, but she was certain of how she felt.

"I, ah, don't have any diseases—had a check-up a few months ago—and I'm on birth control. Are you, um, clean?"

If it had been in any other context, the way T.J. froze mid-movement and went rigid, his gaze flying to her face, might have been comical. As it was, it was hot as hell.

"Yeah, I'm clean. We get tested all the time." His voice sounded strangled. "Are you...? Rose, are you sayin' what I think you are?"

Her cheeks heated, then the rest of her face, until she felt her blush move down to cover her chest as well. "I think you should come back to bed and find out," she managed, but it was enough. With flattering speed, he crossed the room at a pace close to a jog, making his hard cock bob where it thrust out in front of him. She rose to her knees on the bed, so they were face-to-face and she could put her arms over his shoulders, his hardness jutting against her stomach. This time, she started the kiss, and he pulled her closer so that she lost herself in his taste, and the feel of his body against hers, his arms surrounding her. When he finally pulled away — although only a scant inch, so that she could still feel his breath against her wet lips as he spoke — she felt dazed with how cherished and sexy he made her feel.

"Your trust is a beautiful gift, Rose…and I don't take it lightly," he said, his voice low and intent.

His words, and the emotion behind them, warmed her from the inside out.

"Are you sure?" he asked, the tone rough. Any reservations she might have had disappeared in the face of his absolute consideration for her.

She nodded. "Yes," she whispered.

"Thank God," he breathed, his lips twisting into a rueful smile. "I would stop…and I still will, any time you tell me…but the idea of bein' inside you, bare, and fillin' you up…" This time, the sound he made could only be described as a growl. "It's everythin' I've been dreamin' of and more."

She shivered at the rough need she heard behind his words. "Can I…? Is it all right if I touch you?"

He held out his arms to his sides in invitation. "You can do anythin' you want to me, baby…any time." His small smile was wry. "Although I can't promise how long I'll last with you touching me."

She reached out, tentatively stroking him at first so that he shuddered. The idea that she, plain old Rose Abbott, could make such a huge, powerful man tremble with her hand was heady. It made her feel powerful in a way she never had, and she grew bolder, closing her grip around as much of T.J.'s thickness as she could. He felt hot, incredibly hard but with velvety skin, and when she continued the light pressure along his length, his gurgled moan made her pussy give an answering flutter. Another bead of pre-cum oozed from his tip, and he grabbed her wrist.

"I thought I could hold out longer...for you, Rose, but you feel too fuckin' good. I have to be inside you," he rasped, moving one of his own enormous hands to her folds. She was so slick she was practically dripping, and he made a deep sound of satisfaction. "Mmm...you're so wet, honey. Is that cream for me?" he asked, and she nodded, widening her thighs slightly. "I want to hear it out loud, Rose. Tell me you're mine," he demanded, and she felt the same shivery desire in her gut that always went through her when he gave her an order.

"I'm so wet...just for you," she confessed. "*All* for you, because I'm yours," she finished, and there was satisfaction written in his harsh features.

"And I'm yours," T.J. answered, fisting his cock at the same time as he continued to caress her, pushing his fingers into her. She was sopping so that his strokes made a sound, and she blushed.

"Never be embarrassed, darlin'. It's beautiful that you're so aroused. Are you ready to feel your man deep inside that pretty little cunt?"

At his dirty words, and the intensity behind them, Rose's channel clenched again and she felt empty...suddenly desperate for him. "Oh, yes," she answered fervently, and he gently guided her back, falling on top of her.

He stroked his heavy length through the moisture of her slit, over and over, making sure to drag along her clit with every movement until she was breathless and wild. She wrapped her arms and legs around him, pulling his hips against her with her heels on his muscular ass.

"Does that feel good?" T.J. drawled, chuckling as she pushed her hips up to try to get him inside of her.

"More...*more*," she whimpered. She was nearly mindless with desire, but when he notched his thick head at her entrance, she knew an instant of trepidation. As he started to push inside her, though, he went slowly, watching her intently, and she felt cherished all over again. At first, she merely felt a delicious fullness, then a stretch, and when the stretch became almost painful, her breathing sped and grew shallower.

T.J. froze, the muscles of his enormous arms like granite on either side of her. "You okay, baby? Need to stop?" His dark eyes were liquid, and so concerned that she felt warm and gooey.

She considered his question, and the pressure of him inside her, which was starting to go from stretched to intense.

"I think...it's a lot, but it feels good," she answered honestly, even if not totally coherently.

"No matter what we do, I want to make you feel amazin', Rose," he answered, and she tightened around him, making him shudder and groan.

When he bent his head to pull one of her nipples back into the hot cavern of his mouth, she gasped, and felt him slide in just a tiny bit farther.

"Oh, you like that, hmm?" he asked, his dark chuckle loud in the quiet room.

"So...good," she answered, breathless as he licked and sucked her other peak as well. Still going slowly, with his attentions to her nipples, she was shocked when he was fully seated inside of her and she felt nothing but a deep, intense pleasure…beyond anything she'd ever felt before.

T.J. continued his sensual assault on her breasts until she was moaning and clenching around him, making tiny movements with her hips.

"Okay, now, baby?" he asked, his voice strangled. She realized he had been holding himself totally steady, so that his arms were shaking a little, and a wave of warmth for his consideration rose inside her.

"More…than…okay," she managed to huff out, and he began to move. At first, his strokes were slow and shallow, but when she moaned with pleasure, feeling his length drag along every nerve-ending inside of her sheath with aching deliberation, he quickened his pace until he set a steady rhythm.

"You feel…so…fuckin'…spectacular," T.J. grunted in time with his thrusts. "Like you…were…made… for…me."

Her only answer was a low keening as he shifted the angle of his hips, hitting something inside her that made her entire body go crazy with need.

T.J.'s answering grin was feral, and he sped up, making sure to hit the same spot over and over until she was hurtling toward a wall of ecstasy.

"Oh…oh…yes!" she wailed, thrashing her head back and forth on the bed quilt. When he snaked one hand between them to stroke her bundle of nerves, the combination of sensations sent her soaring over the edge of her orgasm, the feeling so intense she thought she might be flying, tensing and bucking underneath him.

For his part, T.J. pushed into her with four more deep strokes until he went rigid, giving a hoarse yell as he emptied himself inside of her with pulse after pulse of his hot seed.

Chapter Thirteen

Nothing—none of his intensive training courses or even the most FUBAR missions—had prepared T.J. for the power of making love to Rose. And he had realized about halfway through that it was what he had been doing...truly *making love*. Somehow, somewhere between reluctantly rising out of the dust with no cover to rescue her and carrying her up the stairs to the Santa Suite of Hunt's Falls' nicest hotel, Rose had climbed into his heart, and he never wanted her to leave.

He eased off her a little bit, astonished at how weak his arms felt and how breathless he remained as they lay, plastered together, still on top of the quilt of the four-poster Victorian bed. The slightest slide of their skin felt amazing, and he could barely hold back his groan. Rose made a little mewl of contentment and he pulled her closer, so that her silky head rested on his chest, right over his heart.

The shadows in the room had lengthened since they'd checked in, and he thought that sunset must be nearly upon them now. The combined scents of cinnamon, clove, nutmeg and pine tickled his nose, but underneath it, the musky scent of Rose's arousal mixed with his essence. It smelled like sex, and he fucking reveled in it. Even now, he could scarcely believe that Rose had not only wanted him inside of her, but also without the barrier of a condom. Her trust and faith in him were enormous, and he silently vowed that he would never betray them.

The object of his thoughts was sighing and cuddling closer next to him.

"You okay, darlin'?" he asked.

He heard a sound suspiciously like a snuffling as she semi-lifted her head, but then must have decided it was too much effort, simply turning to look at him. Her stormy-ocean-blue-eyes were shining.

"Nope... Waaaay better than okay. I'm pretty sure I just died and went to heaven." She sighed again, the sound heavy with contentment. Damned if his cock — which he'd thought would have been satisfied and lazy for at least an hour — didn't twitch with interest.

"Hate to break it to you, sugar, but I'm pretty sure that angels don't do what we just did." He chuckled, and she grinned up at him.

"Well, if they don't, they should. That was... *incredible*." She sounded as if she meant the words, deeply.

Now T.J.'s ego swelled almost as large as his cock had felt a short while earlier. "It was, at that, darlin'," he agreed wholeheartedly. "You sure know how to make me feel like an amazin' lover."

"Well," she hedged, her cheeks going that adorable rosy color that he thought he would likely never grow tired of seeing. "You were...*are* amazing. I've never felt anything like it…the way you, um, you know…at the end?"

His low laughter was a bit smug, but he thought she'd likely forgive him. "The way I made you come so hard you screeched like a banshee?"

She lifted her head worriedly. "No! I didn't… Tell me I didn't do that."

His smile widened to a grin. "You most certainly did, and it was a glorious thing. I'd intended to spend much longer inside you, but I felt the way you clamped down on me, heard your scream and I just lost it." Another worry occurred to him, and he drew his eyebrows together. "Are you… Did I make you sore?" he asked.

Rose traced her fingertips through the whorls of dark hair on his chest. "Maybe just a little—you're really big—but I'll recover," she assured him, then her expression grew mischievous. "And it was totally worth it," she added.

He slapped her ass lightly, loving how the flesh quivered a little bit. The sound was loud in the silent room. "Minx," he scolded mockingly.

Her answering grin was unrepentant, and his heart swelled until he was surprised his chest could still contain it.

"I'll draw you a bath… That should help," he said, torn between satisfaction that she'd enjoyed herself so thoroughly and unease that he'd made her uncomfortable with his size.

"You don't have to do that," she answered.

He leaned closer, kissing her forehead. "I know," he agreed. "But I want to…and I'll call to have two helpin's of that Christmas Eve dinner brought to our room, too, if that sounds good? I was hopin' very much that you'd spend the night."

"Hmm…on one condition," she answered. He was pretty sure she was teasing him, but some of the old insecurities crept back in, just for an instant, and he worried that maybe she hadn't wanted to spend all of Christmas Eve with him. Maybe she wanted them to go back to her friends' house? With surprise, he realized that he would be okay with that…with whatever she wanted. It would be hell to part with her for any length of time again, but he truly cared about making her happy, whatever it took.

"Anythin'," he answered honestly, bracing himself for her reply.

When she looked up at him again, her eyes were dancing with amusement. "You have to wear your Santa hat and nothing else while we eat," she answered, and his bark of laughter filled the room.

"Done… I'll never wear clothes again when we're alone if you'd like, darlin'." He knew he was probably grinning like the fool that he was, but he couldn't help it. He stood and bent over to whisper in her ear before he crossed the room to the bathtub. "*You* can wear whatever you want, sugar, because I'll just take it all off you later."

He loved the way her eyes darkened and goosebumps rose again on her skin. Even better, he could feel her hot gaze on his ass as he went to draw her a proper bath.

* * * *

As they were eating a full Victorian Christmas feast, T.J. sitting next to her on the same side of the large table, Rose reflected that this was quite possibly — *probably* — the best Christmas Eve she'd spent as an adult. In fact, it might be the best ever. She'd texted Heidi earlier to apologize and let her know that she was staying with T.J. for the night, to which her best friend had responded, *'Knew it! Go get 'em, tiger! rawr <3'*.

Next, T.J. had helped her with a hot, relaxing bath, refusing to climb in until he'd thoroughly pampered her by washing her everywhere with long, languid movements. When he'd finally climbed in to soak with her, she'd been so keyed up it had barely taken him a minute to make her come again with those long, talented fingers of his. She felt her cheeks heat at the memory.

She must have made a choking sound because T.J. looked over at her questioningly, his expression of concern transforming to one of sly amusement.

"Penny for your thoughts, honey…or more, if they're naughty," he offered, raising one dark eyebrow. "Maybe you just wanna come over here and sit on my lap so I can feed you some plum puddin'?"

True to his promise, he was naked as a jaybird except for his Santa hat, which he wore at a rakish angle. They'd devoured the roast goose with chestnut dressing, potatoes, asparagus, and grilled carrots, but he'd set the silver-domed serving dish for the plum pudding and hard sauce to one side *"for sharin'"*. The food had been delivered by a merry-looking Mrs. Henderson, who hadn't batted an eyelash at T.J.'s strange attire of only a white robe and the festive hat. In fact, Rose was pretty sure the older woman had been eyeing his chest with appreciation.

And who wouldn't? she wondered. *It is a phenomenal chest.*

"Hmm…I like that look," T.J. continued, recalling her to the present, and the fact that she was ogling him so hard she was surprised her tongue wasn't lolling out of her mouth. *Would he actually mind that?*

"I think Mrs. Henderson was staring at your chest," she blurted out. T.J.'s rich laughter rolled into the room.

"If that's the case—and that's a big '*if*', honey—I can assure you that you have nothin' to worry about, from her or any other woman, for that matter." His chocolate-brown eyes were twinkling but earnest as well. "Was that really what you were thinkin' about when you were blushin', though?" he prodded.

"Well, I was also thinking about how happy I am...which made me remember our bath, earlier..." She trailed off, leaving the rest unsaid, but from the way T.J.'s pupils dilated, she knew he understood the direction of her thoughts.

"Oh yeah?" he prompted, fluttering his fingers over her bare knee, then up her inner thigh in a way that would have been indecent at any restaurant. Her pulse went wild and her breathing quickened.

"In that case, I think you should *definitely* come sit on Santa's lap again, darlin', so I can feed you dessert," he urged, his voice deep and gravelly.

"Don't you want to have any?" she asked.

He narrowed his eyes. "Oh, I'm fixin' to have a treat, too." His answer was so filled with certainty, heavy with innuendo, that her stomach jumped with awareness.

"Oka—" she agreed, squeaking indignantly when he lifted her up and onto him before she had even finished speaking. Still, when he cuddled her into his enormous, warm chest, she couldn't stay too offended.

"Much better," he commented. "I missed you, all the way over there."

She giggled and felt his cock swell underneath her butt with her movements. "From next to you?"

"Pretty sure that any time I'm not touchin' you, you're too far away," he answered, looking for all the world as if he meant it, even though she knew he must be joking with such an outrageous comment.

"How did you survive all these months?" she asked, playing along.

He waited until she turned to look at him before he answered. "Very unhappily," he replied. He shook his head, lifting the fancy dome to reveal the steaming pudding.

Her nose twitched appreciatively. "Mm-m…it smells heavenly! I don't think I've ever had plum pudding, although of course I've heard of it. We were more of a sugar cookies and milk family for the holidays."

"I was on a multi-national mission over Christmas once, with a bunch of British special ops guys. They said it wouldn't be Christmas without pudding for them…and I can assure you, it was surprisingly delicious." His expression took on a far-off cast when he spoke about it.

Rose hated imagining him working over the holidays, in danger. "Where was that?" she asked.

His smile was wry. "Far away," he answered, and she kicked herself for asking. She'd forgotten that he could barely tell her…well, much of anything.

"I'm glad you're safe," she said, her voice low and sincere. "And I'm even more glad that all that happened to you in the past few months was a few new scars…but don't think I didn't notice that some of them look recent." She touched the largest and reddest of his scars, the one that still looked thick and slightly painful.

T.J.'s hand closed over hers, holding her touch to his side. His eyes appeared suspiciously shiny. "Thank you for carin', my lovely Rose. It helped, knowin' I had to get back to you," he answered, and it was like a confession—or maybe more like a vow. She wasn't totally sure what he was vowing, though.

He cleared his throat. "Now, then, why don't you try a bite?" he asked, but it sounded more like a command than a question.

She opened her mouth obligingly, raising one sassy eyebrow, and was shocked when he tore off a piece of the dark brown cake with his fingers and popped it into her mouth. The flavor was spicy, redolent with all the flavors of Christmas, and it was as warm as the dish itself. The texture was spongy and thick, but broken up by plump raisins and boozy orange zest pieces.

"Yumm," she moaned, letting her lips close around his fingers, licking every last crumb off them.

He grunted and shifted underneath her, obviously trying to find a comfortable position for his lengthening erection.

"You are, hands down, the sexiest woman I've ever seen...much less held in my arms," he said, his voice almost harsh with the force of his ardor.

"Do you want some?" she asked innocently, batting her eyelashes. Rose didn't think she'd ever done such a thing in her life...then realized that nobody else had ever *inspired* her to act this way. Only T.J. *Always* T.J.

"Yes, please," he groaned, and she popped a bite of the dessert into his mouth with her fingers. She yelped as he nipped at the tips. When he soothed the sting with his tongue, her breath caught in her throat.

"I don't know how I'm going to survive the hard sauce," she murmured, and his huff of laughter was pure decadence.

"I think you'd better take your sweater off again, darlin'...to keep it clean." He raised that one, roguish eyebrow again and her gut did a little somersault. She let him help her pull her sweater—which was all she had donned for dinner—over her head until her breasts bobbled free, practically in T.J.'s face, due to their positions.

He didn't seem to mind. Quite the contrary, in fact, as his eyes went molten with desire.

"Fuckin' gorgeous," he breathed, his hot breath tickling against her nipples. Reaching around her, he dipped one finger into the warmed ramekin that held the topping for their dessert, then held it to her mouth. She closed her lips around his fingertip and the fiery, sweet decadent taste exploded on her tongue.

"Mm-m...ooh, I like that," she said, barely recognizing the purr in her own voice. T.J. just made a strangled moan in response.

"Please, Santa, can I have some more?" she teased.

"You can have everythin'," he answered, the vibrations from his low voice tickling her side where she was pressed to him. His smile was full of promise, and this time, he scooped even more onto his finger, so that some slid off to land on her bare bosom.

As she licked his forefinger clean once more, he bent his dark head to kiss the sauce off her breasts. All the air left her lungs in a breathless puff as she arched her back, making her full mounds jut practically into his mouth in blatant invitation. He looked up at her with his eyes only, still trailing kisses along her skin, and the erotic image that he presented made her core go liquid with arousal. Absently, she noticed that his dark eyelashes were ridiculously long, and she wanted to feel them against her, too.

"You taste so good like this, honey. Tell me what you want." As T.J. spoke, he reached up to cup her, feathering his thumbs over both nipples.

Holding his gaze, she whispered, "More."

His deep chuckle was indulgent, and he lifted one sardonic eyebrow, but he obliged her by smearing more of the warm, gooey sauce — directly onto her hardened peaks this time. When he sucked them clean again, swirling his tongue around each tip, she couldn't help but clutch at his head to hold him to her, squirming against him so that his cock felt like an iron bar underneath her, pinned between them.

This time, when he lifted his head, his brown eyes blazed. "Are you still tender?" he demanded, his voice harsh with need.

She shook her head. "The bath helped a lot," she answered, her words melting into a shocked gasp as he stood, lifting her along with his motion. She only vaguely heard the chair clatter to the floor behind them as he marched across the room to the bed.

When he set her down near the end with surprising gentleness, she looked back at him questioningly. His muscles were rigid, clearly defined everywhere as if he held himself taut, and his cock? It looked magnificent and swollen, straining toward her.

"Need to feel you again, Rose. Tell me you want me." The words sounded dragged from him, and he reached to cup her mound, teasing one thick finger into her wetness. She could feel how slick she'd gotten from their teasing, and he made a sound of satisfaction. "You're so fuckin' wet, honey. You drive me crazy."

"I want you," she confirmed in a low voice, and his eyes flickered with something hot...dangerous.

"Thank God," he groaned. "Bend over and hold onto the bedpost...just like I've been picturin' you since we stepped through the door."

Her cheeks heated at the erotic image he painted, and she thought maybe she should be shocked, but instead, it only made her more wildly aroused. She obliged him, looking back over her shoulder at him all the while she gripped the thick, mahogany bedpost, with its vertical carvings, and thrust out her ass toward him, parting her thighs.

He fisted his cock as he watched her with avid eyes...and he should have looked ridiculous, still wearing the jaunty Santa hat, but instead he looked like a conqueror of old, barely holding himself back from falling on her like a beast. She shivered and felt more liquid pulse from her channel.

When she braced herself for the fullness of his invasion, he surprised her by instead sinking to his knees behind her, holding her hips as he bent to lap at her slit. It felt amazing—T.J. seemed to know just how to touch her to drive her wild—and she held on to the wooden column like a lifeline as he drove her effortlessly to the brink of orgasm with his talented tongue and fingers.

When he stood abruptly, leaving her right on the edge, she could have cried with disappointment, but it was short-lived when he drove into her with one long stroke, erasing any other thought from her mind.

"Oh God...yes! You feel so big," she panted. It was a full completeness like she'd never experienced, as if she didn't know where T.J. ended and Rose began. She loved it.

"You're so fuckin' tight...slick," he grated out, pushing against her so her breath caught in her throat. "Perfect."

Even through her sensual haze, she couldn't let him think that. "Not perfect," she gasped.

His smile was a hot mixture of tender and sinful. "Perfect for me," he countered, flexing his hips and starting up a slow rhythm, increasing the pace slowly.

"Oh, T.J.... T.J.," she said, not knowing if she was more overcome by the sincerity she'd heard in his voice, or the intensity of him driving into her, each stroke feeling like a reaffirmation.

Where before she'd been holding the bedpost to please him, now she needed it to remain upright. When he curled his body around hers so he could squeeze one of her sensitive nipples at the same time as he brushed a light caress over the nub of her clit, the force of her sudden orgasm took her by surprise. She heard her own scream dimly as every nerve-ending in her body fired at once, launching her into a wave of pure bliss. As if in a dream, she felt T.J. continue pounding into her, his cock making a wet sliding noise with how slick she was. He gave a loud roar as he bucked one last time, shooting jet after jet of molten cream deep into her pussy.

She only vaguely felt him lift her away from the pole before he collapsed behind her on the bed, still curled around her.

* * * *

The profound satisfaction that filled T.J. as he looked down at Rose, sleeping deeply next to him, was unlike anything he'd ever experienced before. He realized that, while he may have been in a committed relationship before—one he never would have betrayed—his feelings for Rose were so much more. What he'd felt for every other woman just paled in comparison.

She stirred and turned toward him dreamily. "T.J.?" she whispered, sounding afraid to believe he was really there.

"Yeah, it's me, darlin'...right here, next to you, holdin' you." His words were a reassuring rumble.

"Missed you," she murmured on a sigh, and his throat felt tight.

"Thought I might never see you again...never find you, or even know what happened," she continued, sounding so sad that it tore at something deep inside him.

"No more secrets, pretty Rose, I promise." He knew she probably wouldn't remember his vow in the morning, but he couldn't help himself.

She smiled, curling into him. His dick, traitor that it was, began to stretch and fill again. He felt a dark amusement that he, who had worried he was a washed-up old has-been, too old for her, was now acting as insatiable as a horny teenager. It was Rose. She drove him absolutely wild for her.

"Stay with me?" Her question was a mere thread of sound, but it bowled him right over—how much he loved hearing it, knowing that for the first time in a very, very long time, he could oblige.

"Of course, darlin'. You just go to sleep, and I'll be here in the mornin'," he reassured her, his voice cracking. If he held her tighter than he needed to, that was just between him and Rose.

Chapter Fourteen

When T.J. cracked his eyes open, he could tell from the dim light that it was scarcely past dawn. The sensation of waking up in a strange place had become so common for him as to be familiar, but the odd surge of excitement—no, *anticipation*—was new. It was far from unwelcome, though.

When he looked down at the gorgeous woman in his arms, flushed and well-loved, all the memories of the night before flooded back in a rush, and he felt so full he might burst with it. As if she sensed his gaze, Rose's eyes fluttered open and she turned to look at him with a muzzy expression, which morphed into a shy smile.

"Morning... Merry Christmas," she said in a voice still husky with sleep. It was unbelievably sexy.

"Good mornin', sugar, and Merry Christmas to you, too," he answered, pulling her the rest of the few inches that separated them to kiss her.

She made a muffled sound of protest. "I might have morning breath!" she managed to get out, but he shook his head.

"Don't care," he returned, unable to keep his hands from stroking everywhere he could touch. Her skin was like satin, and gorgeously luminous in the early-morning light. "Wanna kiss you always…in a cave, in a carriage, at night, in the morning…*always*." He kissed around her face, each corner of her mouth, until she opened for him, and they were both lost in the embrace for a long moment.

The interlude was broken, however, when Rose's stomach gave a loud grumble. She looked abashed, and his bark of laughter filled every corner of the hushed room.

"Sounds like I need to feed you before I do anything else, hmm?" he teased.

"Well, can you blame me for working up an appetite?" she returned, her sparkling gray-blue eyes holding a saucy glint.

He chuckled, realizing that he didn't think he'd smiled or laughed this much in years. *Have I* ever *laughed this much?* he wondered. He loved his unit, and they were like brothers, ribbing and teasing one another whenever they got the chance. He would die for them. In fact, he almost had…several times over.

But Rose? She was like pure sunshine, illuminating every dim corner inside of him until he felt her joy just radiating right through him. Even as a child — burdened by heavy responsibility and danger at home — he'd never felt this incandescent buoyancy.

He was so lost in thought that it took him a moment to realize that she was looking nervous, as if she wanted to ask him something but wasn't certain of his response.

"We…well, we're invited to Christmas morning with Heidi and Edie, and dinner with Heidi's parents and brother, too. They…they've always been like a second family for me and Alec, especially since our granny passed." She bit her lip. "I mean, if you have time? I understand, no matter what."

Looking at the way she lowered her eyes, hiding behind her thick, light-brown lashes, a shade darker than her hair…noting how she held herself uncomfortably, pulling the sheet up to cover her stunning curves, T.J. felt a pinch in the region of his heart. *How have I been such an idiot not to make everything clear to her?* he chastised himself. Even as he did, he knew the answer. He'd been worried about protecting himself, when he should have made things obvious from the get-go. *No more,* he vowed.

He stood abruptly, and Rose's eyes widened when she saw how hard he was already for her.

He gestured toward his groin. "Don't worry, darlin'. This happens all the time around you. It'll settle down…probably."

He picked up his jeans from the floor, hopping a bit to tug them on in his haste. "Stay here, just like you are. I'll be right back…I promise. I have somethin' for you — somethin' I hope you'll like."

Her full pink lips formed a little moue of surprise. "O-okay," she stammered, watching him get dressed at record speed. He couldn't help but press a kiss to her startled mouth — she was so fucking irresistible — before he rushed out of the room.

Is T.J. coming back? she wondered, cutting off the worry immediately as unworthy toward him. He had said he'd return shortly, and while she knew there was a lot he couldn't tell her, he'd been honest about having secrets from the beginning. She lay back and snuggled into the pillows, inhaling deeply when she noticed that traces of his distinctive scent still lingered. *Last night was incredible*, she mused, feeling almost moony with happiness. *T.J. was – is – incredible, and he chose to be with me.* She felt the familiar flutter of butterflies in her stomach, something only thoughts of T.J. seemed to bring out in her.

She decided to wait patiently, as he'd requested, but she figured she had enough time to run to the bathroom before he returned. She was just resettling under the covers, feeling decadently naked, when the door to the room burst open with a blast of cooler air.

As T.J. crossed quickly to her side, kissing her thoroughly, she could see tiny little snowflakes caught in his hair and on his shoulders, and smell the faint traces of fresh snow and cold clinging to him.

When he broke off the kiss, she was breathless and blushing. "What was that for?" she asked.

His grin was unrepentant. "You looked so sexy that I just couldn't help myself." He held up a paper bag and dug an envelope out of the shoulder bag he carried as well.

"Here's the breakfast of pastries Mrs. Henderson left for us downstairs with a little note," he started, jiggling the paper bag to it crinkled.

"Aw, that was so sweet of her!" Rose exclaimed. "What did the note say?"

T.J.'s expression grew bashful, and his ears turned red. "She, uh, she's happy I seem to be taking such good care of you," he stammered, and Rose looked at him curiously. It sounded innocuous enough. Why was he so embarrassed?

She forgot her lingering questions, though, when he knelt next to the bed and thrust the envelope toward her.

"Merry Christmas, darlin'. Here's your gift," he said gruffly, but his eyes belied his tone. He was trying to sound as if it didn't matter much, but his chocolate-brown eyes were hopeful and worried all at once. Whatever this was, it was important to him.

He shrugged off his coat, letting it fall to a heap behind him, and set his bag on the floor as he watched her open it.

Rose slid the single sheet of paper out of the envelope, noting that it appeared to be an official confirmation of some sort, from the United States government. As she skimmed each line, excitement bubbled up into her chest.

When she looked at his face—with his prominent nose and rough features, which had become so very important and beloved to her—his image wavered a bit as her eyes stung and her throat felt tight. "Is this...is this what I think it is?"

"If you think it's my last set of orders, for a final three months as a trainer in Wisconsin before I retire, then...yes?" He made it a question, watching her so intently she knew that he was gauging every nuance of her expression.

"And...you wanted to retire?" She knew what she hoped his answer was, but she didn't want to assume.

He stroked a finger from her cheekbone to her chin and he smiled so that the corners of his eyes crinkled. "I put in my request as soon as I could after leavin' you. I..." He took a deep, fortifying breath. "I never want to leave you again for longer than I have to. I'm hopin'—*prayin'*—that you feel the same way. I love you, Rose."

Aurora Russell

The last part came out in a rush, but she heard and treasured every word.

"Oh, T.J.! Yes!" she said. Forgetting that she was still naked, she leaped off the bed to throw her arms around him, knocking him backward so he landed on his butt with a startled '*Oof*', which turned into a deep chuckle.

"I love you, too," she said, feeling his arms close around her so that her cheek pressed right up against the hollow of his neck. "I'm in awe of everything that you do...that you've done for our country...but is it horrible if I admit that I'm thrilled you'll be retiring?"

He looked down his impressive nose at her. "Not a bit... That's exactly how I dreamed you'd feel, honey," he answered, kissing her again, more deeply this time, so that she was warm and breathless by the time the embrace ended. She could feel his now-familiar hardness growing against her, and she wiggled, enjoying the way he groaned as his eyes darkened.

"Do you think we have some time before your friends expect us for Christmas mornin'?" he drawled, palming the globes of her ass so that her inner channel clenched.

"Definitely," she agreed, although she suspected she wouldn't have cared if they'd been hours late. She was so filled with happiness, finally able to be with her secret Santa forever.

"Then let's find some mistletoe so you can tell me where you want me to kiss you, hmm?" T.J. teased, raising his eyebrows.

* * * *

"So, spill!" Heidi urged as soon as Rose was alone with her in the kitchen, getting more drinks for

157

everyone. "That man can't take his eyes off you. Was last night amazeballs?" She pulled a carafe of fresh-squeezed orange juice along with a bottle of champagne out of the fridge. "Who am I kidding? Look at the glow in your cheeks. *Of course* it was!" she finished, answering her own question

Rose felt her face flame. "We... Last night was phenomenal. Then..." She sighed, still afraid to trust how happy she felt.

"Then what? You're killin' me, Abbott!" Heidi complained, but she was smiling, her short hair as wild as usual.

"Then he told me that he loves me...and we'll be free to be together full-time in three months when he's officially retired." Rose sighed with elation.

Heidi set the bottles down hard on the granite countertop and squeezed her in a tight bearhug. "Oh, Rosie...I'm so frickin' happy for you! You deserve *all* the love."

Rose felt a lump in the back of her throat at the affection she heard in her best friend's tone. "Thanks, Hy," she answered, hugging her back.

They were both surprised when they heard the doorbell ring. Rose looked at Heidi quizzically.

"You expecting someone else? I thought your brother was meeting us at your parents' later?" Rose asked.

"Beats me," Heidi answered, looking curious. "Oooh! Maybe it's a special gift! Although I always feel so horrible for everyone who has to work on Christmas."

Rose raised her eyebrows, and they abandoned their mimosa ingredients to go to the front door.

"Who was it?" Heidi asked.

Edie shrugged. "There was nobody there, but there was a gift."

It was only then that Rose noticed that T.J. was holding a fancy stocking with a bemused expression. The decoration had '*Hook & Rose*' embroidered on it.

"Must be for me," he answered, reaching into the toe and pulling out a note and a small black, velvet box...like a fancy jewelry box.

Heidi was nearly bouncing on her feet as he read, impatient as always. "Well, don't keep us hanging, man! What does it say?"

T.J.'s expression was intense, and he looked directly as Rose when he replied. If they'd been alone, she thought he might have carried her off to the bed again.

"It says, '*Merry Christmas. We thought you might be needing this under the mistletoe.*'" His voice was deep and rumbling, and before she knew it, she'd crossed the room to stand before him.

"What's in the little box?" She whispered the question, hope and excitement rising as she saw her own feelings mirrored on T.J.'s face.

"Why, I do believe it's most likely my grandmother's engagement ring, which my unit brothers must have gotten from my little sister," he said, cracking the box open a tiny bit, wonder in his tone.

When he fell to one knee before her, her heart flew right up into her throat.

"Rose Abbott, you're the light and joy and beauty I didn't know I was missin' until I tackled you to the ground, and I never want to be apart from you again. You don't have to answer right now—I'll wait as long as you want, years even, for you to decide—but I want you to know how serious I am about you, about us." He looked up at her with hope and love shining in his gleaming eyes, and she felt as though they were the only two people on the planet at the moment.

He took a deep breath before he continued. "Will you make me the happiest of men, and consider marryin' me?"

Rose knew it was fast in terms of how many days they'd spent together, but she'd felt the instant connection with him the moment they'd met, and it had only deepened over their months apart, cemented by their explosive, magical reunion. She didn't need more time. She was sure.

"Yes," she answered. "With you, T.J., my answer will always be yes."

Beaming crookedly, he jumped to his feet, and she vaguely heard Heidi and Edie squealing and clapping, but she only had eyes for the tough, scarred secret special forces operative who was now all hers.

Sliding the ring onto her finger, he brought it to his lips, kissing her hand with exquisite tenderness. "I love you so much, darlin'," he whispered, sounding suspiciously hoarse.

She lifted up onto her tiptoes to press a kiss to his lips. "Love you, too…forever and always."

Want to see more from this author? Here's a taster for you to enjoy!

Sheltered by the Soldier
Aurora Russell

Excerpt

His favorite nurse was back. He didn't even have to see her — he could tell by her quiet voice, speaking low to the other nurses and staff, and by the slow, almost hesitant tread of her steps. She'd been gone for two days, and he'd been worried when one of the others had told him she was out sick. She sounded like she was feeling better now…although her laugh had a brittle edge to it. He'd spent seemingly endless hours observing, watching and assessing other people — it was part of what made him such a damn good operative — and while she disguised it well, Nurse Carraday was hiding something.

That wasn't why he liked her so much, although he had never been able to resist a mystery. No, he liked her because she had gentle hands that she always tried to warm before she touched him, she laughed at his terrible jokes, and she blushed every time she walked into his room. He enjoyed her witty commentary, even when she spoke it nearly under her breath, and he appreciated how she'd opened up and told him about being raised by a single mom, something they had in common, except her momma had passed two years earlier. He especially loved the warmth in her manner, how she seemed to bring more light into the room. There was nothing remotely inappropriate in her conduct, and he made sure that his actions were above reproach, but…she made him dream again.

As if on cue, she slipped into his room with silent steps that would have done a Navy SEAL proud, and her cheeks grew rosy as she gave him a tremulous smile.

"Nurse Carraday, I was gettin' mighty worried about you." *Brian, that was pretty damn obvious of you*, he scolded himself. The pretty young nurse seemed to agree.

"I'm just fine, Mr. Clark, not that it's any of your business," she answered in that prim, starchy tone that drove him crazy. "It's nice of you to say so, though," she added, her eyes softening, and he thought she wouldn't like how much she revealed with her small gestures. She would make a terrible poker player, and that was the Lord's own truth.

"I'm glad," he answered warmly, and he could see from the rapid rising and falling of her chest under her plain scrubs that her breath quickened.

As she leaned over to take his temperature and set the blood pressure cuff, he got a faint whiff of something fruity. He knew from one of his sisters who worked in the medical field that nurses weren't allowed to wear perfume, so he assumed it was her shampoo or soap. Whatever it was, it smelled like sunshine…clothes out drying on the line, or picking warm peaches straight off of the trees in his family's sprawling backyard.

"I'm sorry, but I have to check your dressings and my hands are cold," she apologized, rubbing them together rapidly. She had beautiful fingers, long and elegant.

Aw, man, Clark, you have it bad, he scolded himself. *Noticing a woman's fingers?* Surely it was a sign of complete obsession. Of course, the rest of her was lovely, too. She was petite but curvy, rounded in all of the right places, and every so often she would unintentionally brush against him. He wished she would give him a chance to feel even a hint of the soft-looking bounty of her full breasts, but he contented himself with the occasional side bump instead. *Yep, totally gone.*

She finished her check efficiently, and her swift nod was satisfied. If he hadn't been studying her movements so closely — okay, *avidly*, like the big bad wolf ready to devour Little Red Riding Hood in a whole different way — he might have missed the marks on her forearm as the sleeve of her lab coat pushed back. She'd skillfully covered the purple smudges with makeup, but he could still make out the faint traces of bruises. No, *shit*, not just bruises…*fingermarks.*

His gaze flashed to hers and she held his stare for a long, fraught moment. At first, she looked stricken, embarrassed, as she adjusted the cuff clumsily. When she met his gaze again, though, there was a sort of haunted, hunted look behind her melting chocolate brown eyes. She was teetering on the brink of flight, and it wouldn't take much to push her over the edge. For his part, Brian felt an unreasoning fury swell inside of his chest, threatening to consume him. Only by pulling on every scrap of his training, every ounce of discipline, did he manage not to say something that would surely drive her away. "Who hurt you?" he asked.

"It's nothing," she whispered.

"Darlin', someone hurting you, puttin' his hands on you…that's *not* nothing." He tried to keep his voice calm, but it was low with fury. Not at her, but at whoever had hurt her. Still, she flinched.

"*Please...*" She begged him with her eyes. "If you make a big deal out of it, I'll have to stay away from here...from you. And I don't want to because...I've been so happy this past week."

Part of him sang at her unconscious admission, but the other part was still just too worried and angry.

"I wondered if you felt it too," he answered quietly.

She laid her hand on top of his, the pressure featherlight, but it was the first time she'd deliberately touched him outside of the context of her duties and it sent a jolt of awareness through him.

"Yes...my gosh, *yes*. Talking with you, joking, laughing...I feel like you *see* me. It's the first time in so long...but spending time with you made me realize how isolated I've become, how frightened." She plucked nervously at the scratchy hospital bedsheet, half-turning her head as if she expected someone to be watching her. It made his heart hurt.

"Oh, I see you, honey, and I love the view."

His audacious comment surprised a huff of laughter out of her, so he continued.

"Conversations with you have been the best part of my days. It's funny, but in spite of how piss-poor I was feeling, especially when I first got here, and being the least active I've been in, well, *ever*—so I openly acknowledge I don't think I've been the best patient" — he raised his eyebrows and gave her a self-deprecating grin—"in spite of all that, I've been feeling this crazy spark whenever we talked. I just assumed maybe it was one-sided, or even if it wasn't, that you weren't free."

She pulled her hand back. "I'm *not* free...and I never thought I would break my promises to my husband but, for the first time in so long, I'm not just resigned to marking the time, letting the days pass by. You make me want to try again, Brian."

"If he's hurtin' you, he doesn't deserve your loyalty," Brian answered, feeling the words deeply. "A real man doesn't ever lay a hand on those weaker than he is, and avoids fighting with everyone else, too."

She quirked her mouth into a half-smile. "Funny philosophy for a former soldier...and a very brave security officer, too, from what I hear. I don't think you got your injuries meditating."

He chuckled. "No indeed, ma'am, but I was protecting someone else."

"Yes, those two stunning young women who came to visit you," she replied with a snap.

He was delighted at her show of jealousy. "They don't hold a candle to you, honey," he answered earnestly.

She flushed bright red, but she looked pleased.

He thought about what she'd said earlier. "Wait a second...you just called me Brian. Does that mean I get to call you Christine now?"

She pursed her lips, making a show of thinking it over. "Hm...I don't know. I don't let just anyone use my first name, you know? Everyone says I'm an old battle-axe on the ward."

His bark of amusement echoed in the quiet room. "Battle-axe? Honey, you're not even a butter knife."

Her answering smile was large and genuine.

His mood darkened again as she reached up to tuck a wisp of hair, one that had escaped her ponytail, behind her ear and her cuff fell again to expose her wrist.

"Let me help you," he said, his voice low and intense. "I may not be at my best right now, but I'm still someone any man would think twice about crossing, and I have friends —"

"He's too dangerous — and crazy — even for you and your friends. He's a police officer so he has enormous resources and power." She leaned closer as she cut him off, her voice barely more than a whisper. "I don't want you to get hurt, but I have a plan. I'm leaving tonight."

Brian's senses went on high-alert.

"Tonight?" he echoed, and Christine nodded urgently, glancing at the clock in front of his bed with dismay.

"Oh, darn it…I have to leave now or I'll be late for my next patient."

He put out a staying hand, wishing he were healing faster. The doctors had marveled at his quick recovery, but now he longed to be at full force so he could take the worry away for the sweet young nurse who'd come to mean so much to him in such a short time.

"Please, I can help. Let me call my friends…or at least one friend. Barnes and I are like brothers, served side-by-side. I'd trust him with my life, my *momma's* life. Danger doesn't bother us one bit."

Christine was already shaking her head. "It's too risky for you to get involved. I have to go alone for my plan to work, and no trace can lead back to you." She shivered so hard he felt it, even with his gentle touch. She glanced at the clock again and Brian had the curious sensation that everything was riding on the next moment, and she was slipping away.

"Let me give you one thing, then. Promise me you'll keep it with you, no matter what."

Christine turned back, studying his expression as if she could see right into his soul. "I promise," she agreed finally.

He grabbed the pen and notepad that he always kept on his bedside table, and wrote down a long series of numbers, folding it rapidly into a small square packet before he handed it to her.

"What is that?" she asked.

He squeezed her hand, pressing the paper into her palm. "It's my secret code. You dial that number on any phone, anywhere, and it will connect directly to me, untraceable."

She looked skeptical. "Really?"

"Honey, you call that number when you're safe, whenever that is. I'll be counting the days." He held her gaze, willing her to see how serious he was, before he continued. "But if anything goes wrong, I swear to you, if you ever need me, call this number, and I *will. Be. There.*"

Hope and doubt warred in her eyes, which grew shiny. She turned away without a word. Brian let her go, figuring he'd pushed her far enough for the moment.

* * * *

At the time she was due to come back later that afternoon, another nurse arrived in her place. Delia, he thought her name was, with long, dark hair that she always wore in intricate braids.

"Where's Nurse Carraday?" he asked. He had seen the two women talking, and they seemed like friends…or friendly, at the very least.

Delia looked worried and his heart gave a double-beat, fit to leap out of chest like it hadn't been since he'd finished his special ops training.

"I'm not sure. She was called away suddenly…some sort of emergency at home with her husband."

Even as he called in every favor that he could, Brian knew it would be useless. Christine Carraday had disappeared.

* * * *

Eight months later

"I like excitement as much as the next ghost — hell, probably like it a lot more — but it'll be good to finally get some real down time. This mission has been nucking futz since we first went wheels-up back in Boston." Tim Barnes grinned and shoved clothes into his go-bag with wanton abandon. "Where're you headed, Castellano? Back home to Wisconsin? What the hell do you even have in Wisconsin other than cheese and beer?"

It was a common joke between the three of them since Castellano had joined their small crew a few months back, working as undercover security guards on an operation with the wealthy and powerful Gaspard family. The younger man shrugged good-naturedly.

"What the hell else do you *need* in life besides cheese and beer? Oh, and beautiful women, of course," Castellano countered.

Barnes chuckled. "Hey!" He nudged Brian with his shoulder. "Tell Castellano that he can't count his mother or his sister when he talks about beautiful women...and since that's half the female population under sixty of his Podunk hometown — "

Brian smiled when Castellano swung a fake punch — or, judging by the loud "*oof*" his friend made when the blow connected, maybe not-so-fake punch — at Barnes.

"I'm never letting you video-chat with my family again," Castellano grumbled.

Brian stepped between them. The tension was partly joking, but it also felt half-way genuine.

"Heyo, Barnes...man, you know it's off-limits to talk about our ladies that way. If you made a comment about one of my sisters, I'd be serving you your balls for breakfast," Brian said.

Barnes smiled, but it didn't entirely reach his eyes. "Fair enough...not that I *would* talk about your sisters, who are perfectly, disgustingly, blissfully happy with their husbands. Do your brothers-in-law even understand what lucky S.O.B.'s they are?"

Brian was happy to go along with the slight change of subject. "Oh, don't you worry...my momma and my sisters remind them regularly." He paused to neatly fold and stow the last of his own gear, wishing he didn't feel such a pang of envy lately when he thought of how happy his sisters were with their husbands. "Castellano's headed to the great Cheeseland Beyond the Wall...where're you traveling? Home to Wyoming?"

Barnes shrugged nonchalantly but his movements betrayed a slight uneasiness. "Might as well make my dad happy, right? And I'll see Sheena, too...if she hasn't given up on me entirely by now."

Sheena was Barnes's high school sweetheart. He carried pictures of her everywhere they went. One drunken night at a bar in Bogota, Barnes had confessed to Brian that he suspected she'd been cheating on him over the years—a lot—but he wasn't sure he wanted to know. Brian didn't blame him.

He clapped his hand on the other man's shoulder. "Good luck, man."

Castellano was equally sympathetic. "I know how that goes. They love the uniform, they think it's so glamorous to be with a hero, but they sure don't love it much when you have to run out in the middle of the night and can't call you for weeks or months. That's why there sure as shit ain't no pretty young thing waiting for me...or at least, she doesn't *know* she's waiting for me yet." He waggled his eyebrows and they all laughed.

He turned to Brian. "What about you, Clark? You got some sweet little beauty pining away for you in South Carolina? Or is it true you're hung up on Clothilde Gaspard?"

Christine's petite form, with chocolate-brown eyes, sprang to Brian's mind but he pushed it down ruthlessly. He'd searched everywhere for her, even trying to track her husband to find her, but it was as if she'd vanished off the surface of the Earth. He refused to let his thoughts go to a darker place.

"Naw, man...I'm going to see my momma and my sisters. Lizzy just had another baby. I'm looking forward to beach days, zoo trips, and a hell of a lot of piggy-back rides for my nieces and nephews." He stepped closer to the younger man. "I am not, and have never been, hung up on Clothilde...and thank God. I know we all like and respect the hell out of Constantin, but he's one scary-ass motherfucker." Marc Constantin was their commanding officer, and madly in love with Clothilde Gaspard.

There was a faint sound of a horn honking, and Barnes heaved his bag onto his back. "That's my ride...you headed to the airport right now, too?" he asked Castellano. The man nodded, and they looked questioningly at Brian.

"My train's later, so I'll see you both on the flipside," he said by way of an answer.

Castellano gave a half-salute.

"You take care," Barnes answered.

With the two other men gone, the small barracks felt cavernous, the silence extra-noticeable after their good-natured ribbing. The sudden buzz coming from his bag sounded loud, and he expected to see his momma's name on the caller-ID. '*No matter how old you get, you'll still always by my sweet baby boy,*' she liked to say. He curved his mouth into a smile that turned to a frown at the nonsense code he saw on the screen instead. It looked like one of the crazy routings favored by Uncle Sam, but as of this morning he was supposed to be on leave—real leave with no chance of getting called in. With an inward sigh, he reminded himself that such a leave didn't exist. Men like him—like Constantin, Barnes and Castellano too—were always on call until they retired or died.

It wasn't his C.O.'s voice giving him orders on the other end of the line, though. It sounded like a woman breathing…no, *crying*. His hand shook as he held the specialized, secure SAT-phone.

"Brian?" she whispered.

It was her. Thank all that was holy, it was *her*. He sat down heavily on the creaking bottom bunk.

"It's me, darlin'. Are you safe?"

Her inhale was shaky. "I'm okay for now, I think, but…he found me. He found me again and I didn't know what else to do. I didn't believe you would actually answer."

"You did the right thing, honey. Just tell me where you are, or where you want to meet, and I will get there."

"Aren't you angry at me? For disappearing then not calling until months later?"

The uncertainty in her voice was ripping up his insides. "No…no, I am most certainly not angry. That's not even in my top three right now. I'm relieved, first and foremost, and happy…and I suppose I'm grateful. We can't talk long on this line, though, so if you could tell me where to go, I will prove to you how not-angry I am."

Her laugh was watery, and he could practically hear the moment she decided to take a chance on him.

"It's a cave behind a biker bar in New Hampshire…the Freedom Lives." He was glad he was sitting down as relief coursed through him. She trusted him, and she was closer than he'd imagined.

"I know that place. I'll be no more than two hours, darlin'. Can you hold on that long?" He mentally ran through the list of friends and brothers who he could call who might be closer…and it was a damn short list. Still, even if they couldn't get to her, he knew Barnes and Castellano would still turn around and help with everything else in a heartbeat.

"I think so," she said quietly. "But…could you please hurry?"

About the Author

Aurora is originally from the frozen tundra of the upper-Midwest (ok, not frozen all the time!) but now loves living in New England with her real-life hero/husband, two wonderfully silly sons, and one of the most extraordinary cats she has ever had the pleasure to meet. But she still goes back to the Midwest to visit, just never in January.

She doesn't remember a time that she didn't love to read, and has been writing stories since she learned how to hold a pencil. She has always liked the romantic scenes best in every book, story, and movie, so one day she decided to try her hand at writing her own romantic fiction, which changed her life in all the best ways.

Aurora loves to hear from readers. You can find her contact information, website details and author profile page at https://www.totallybound.com

Home of Erotic Romance

Sign up for our newsletter and find out about all our romance book releases, eBook sales and promotions, sneak peeks and FREE romance books!